For Dad,
with lots of love

Acknowledgments

Deepest thanks, once again, to my brilliant editor, Liesa Abrams, and my spectacular agent, Jill Grinberg. You two are the best!

Thanks to all the fab folks at Aladdin, including Fiona Simpson, Bess Braswell, Venessa Williams, Bernadette Cruz, Stasia Kehoe, and Jessica Handelman.

Zahra Mirjehan Baird, you're the coolest librarian on the planet, and we're so lucky to have you. Bell Middle School super English teacher Dylan Gilbert, thanks for sharing those fascinating theater improv books!

A big xoxo to all my reader pals. I cherish every single e-mail and letter you send me, and I promise to always write you back!

Mom and Dad, thanks for rearranging the shelves at Barnes & Noble. And rah-rah for the home team: Alex, Josh, Lizzy—and always, Chris, my first reader and number one everything. I love you all!

Sleepwalking

I am standing outside homeroom in yellow flannel monkey pajamas.

Everyone else is dressed normally: jeans, track pants, sweaters, whatever.

Apparently because today, Monday, February 23, is not Pajama Day at Crampton Middle School. Also apparently I am the only one who is celebrating Pajama Day, because I am the only one whose mother *told* her it was Pajama Day. After using the New Student Information Packet to line a dog crate for this one-eared beagle she's babysitting.

"Hey, Marigold," some girl across the hall is calling.

"That's your name, right? Um, no offense, but why are you in your pj's?"

I don't answer. That's because my ears are burning and my eyebrows are sweating. It's hard to say something casual and jokey like *whoops, silly me* with sweaty eyebrows. I dig my thumbnails into my palms, but I'm not waking up.

Now this buzz-cut–headed eighth-grade boy is starting to laugh. And point. "Yo, New Girl. Yeah, you. Did you forget something? *Like getting dressed?*"

That's it; I'm done. I escape from homeroom. My poofy blue bedroom slippers skid on the waxy floor. "Excuse me, no running," some office lady calls out from down the hallway. Which is when I start to run, seeing a mob of giggling girls turning the corner and coming toward me.

I bang open the door to the girls' room and hide myself in a stall. Then I yank my cell phone out of my backpack and speed-dial Mom.

It rings five times. Six times means I'll get her voice mail, which means she'll never get my message, because she doesn't ever check her voice mail. *Pick up*, I pray. *Pick up, pickuppickuppickup.*

"Hello?" she finally shouts. "Marigold?"

Then a truck honks. Right in my ear.

"Mom?" I say.

"Oh, sweetheart, what's wrong? Are you okay?"

"No." I wipe my sweaty face on my flannel arm. "I'm wearing pajamas."

"I know. Those cute monkey ones."

"Because you said it was Pajama Day."

"Right, it is. I read it in the packet."

"Except it isn't."

"It's not Pajama Day? Are you sure? The first day of—what do they call it? Spirit Week?" I can hear dogs barking now. She must be downtown with her Morning Walkers.

"No, it's not," I say loudly. "I'm the only one in the entire school wearing pj's. I look like a total dork."

"I'm sure you don't, baby."

"I'm sure I do. I'm coming home."

"Oh, Mari. You can't."

"Why not?"

"Because you just got there five minutes ago."

That's so illogical I can't even argue. "Okay, then can you please bring me some other clothes?"

"Yes, of course." She shouts this over yapping and arfing dogs. "But you're going to have to wait a few minutes."

"How come?"

"Because I'm not home. I'm at least a mile away, with three of my Walkers. And I'm supposed to pick up two new greyhounds by eight o'clock."

"But this is a major emergency." I check my watch: three minutes until homeroom. "Can't the greyhounds wait?"

"Oh, come on now, Mari," she says in a voice meant to be soothing. Except you can't soothe when you're shouting; it kind of spoils the effect. "So you're wearing pajamas. Have fun with it; improvise. Pretend you're sleepwalking."

"*What?*"

"See where it takes you. Think of it as a costume."

"I don't wear costumes."

"Oh, sure you do, baby. We all do. Every single day."

"Mom," I say. "Can we *please* not have a big philosophical discussion about this?"

"Sorry." A truck honks. "Well, look at it this way. At least you'll be comfortable."

That's when the door to the girls' room creaks open. I can hear the sound of heels on the floor tiles, and then the sharp click of someone locking another stall door. "Just listen to me, okay?" I whisper desperately into my cell. "I *won't* be comfortable. I'll be the *opposite* of comfortable. I'll be traumatized for the *entire rest of my life*. Just please, please bring me different clothes. *Please*. I'm begging you."

She processes. A dog arfs. Finally she says, "All right, I'll be there in a few minutes. BEEZER, SIT. I'm not fooling, buddy. SIT. Good dog."

"Mom? MOM?"

"Just try to hang in there, Mari, okay? First I need to get the greyhounds."

The line goes dead, as if everything's settled. Whatever; at least I got through to her. Mom usually does better in person, but even then, normal back-and-forth conversations are definitely not her strong point.

I leave my stall and check myself out in the mirror. Great. My cheeks are flushed, my eyes look huge and freaked-out, and my wavy brown hair is damp and limp.

Plus, of course, there's the jammie issue. Can't forget that.

I drown my face in freezing water, then crank out some paper towel. The other bathroom user shuffles her feet. Which, I suddenly notice, are in pointy-toe black leather boots. Scary boots. Get-out-of-my-face boots.

I cram the paper towel into the trash can. "Well, bye," I call out, so that at least Pointy Boots knows that I realize she's an earwitness.

"See you, Marigold," Pointy Boots answers in a quiet, amused sort of voice.

No Problem

Samuel J. Crampton Middle is my third school in four years. And if there's one thing I've learned about middle school by now, it's this: Attention is bad. Any attention. And now here I am in seventh-grade homeroom with, like, thirteen girls crowding around my desk, all paying attention to my dorky monkey pajamas.

"Omi*god*, Marigold," says this tall one named Jada Sperry. She has perfectly straight dark blond hair with no split ends, and hyper-sympathetic brown eyes. As far as I can tell, she's in charge. I mean, of *everything.* "What happened? Did you think it was Spirit Week? That was last month!"

"I know. I guess I read the calendar wrong."

"Omigod, I feel so, so sorry for you! What a total nightmare."

"Thanks."

"You must want to die. Omigod, if it was *me*—"

"It wouldn't be you, Jada," says this girl named Ashley with curly brown hair and green rubberbands in her braces. "You'd never mix up the month."

"Hey, everybody makes mistakes," Jada says seriously, and all the other girls nod, like, *Ooh Jada, you're so understanding.*

Then this thick-looking boy named Brody comes up behind me, pokes my shoulder, and snores into my ear: *HONK-Schwee, HONK-Schwee.* He leans over my desk; I can smell his minty toothpaste. "Hey, Marigold, want a bedtime story? And your teddy bear? And a nice glass of milk?"

"Go. Away," Jada says, giving him a look. "He's such a loser, Marigold. Just ignore him."

"Thanks," I say. I'm starting to figure it's my best line in this scene, so I'll just keep saying it until everyone leaves my desk.

And miraculously it works. After another round of Jada announcing to everyone how *sorry* she feels for me, she finally takes her seat. Then Ashley does, and then this superskinny girl named Megan does, and then all the others take theirs. One girl named Layla with smudgy mascara and a bright orange streak in her hair is curled up in her chair and staring at me in a rude-curious sort of way, kind of like a nasty cat, but at least no one's crowding my desk anymore. Maybe, I tell myself, if I just keep acting grateful and boring and monosyllabic they'll forget I'm even here.

Another poke from behind. I spin around, but it's not that moron Brody again. It's this teeny pale girl with big eyes, who I'm pretty sure is named Quinn. "Do you want to borrow my sweater?" she asks in a voice so quiet I can barely hear her. I tell her no because I'd probably be roasting, but thanks for the offer. She looks embarrassed. Maybe I should just take her baby-blue, doll-size sweater, I think, even though there's no way it would fit over my baggy pj's.

I'm about to turn around to ask for it when Mr. Hubley the homeroom/science teacher says in this really juicy, phlegmy voice, "Attendance, please. Settle down." Nobody's listening, so he tries again: "ATTENDANCE, PLEASE. SETTLE YOURSELVES DOWN, PEOPLE." The louder he talks, the juicier he sounds, and he doesn't even bother to clear his throat. *Oh help,* I think. Because what if this isn't a cold, and he's just going to sound like this for the entire rest of the year? If that's the case, I'm not sure I'll pass homeroom, and let's not even discuss science.

He starts calling out names, so to distract myself from his drippy voice I stare at the second hand on my watch: 8:10 and 32 seconds, 8:10 and 33. Mom said she was picking up the new dogs at eight, which was, like, eleven minutes ago, so where is she? Of course, she said they were greyhounds, which means they're probably impossible to walk with a bunch of normal-size Walkers. I try to think who else is on Mom's Morning Walk list this week—Beezer the beagle, Tristan the mutt, Darla the shepherd-something-mix. Nobody too alpha, so hopefully they're getting along okay. Probably she's just crossing a street somewhere, trying to coordinate five leashes without getting herself all tangled up the way she always does. She pretty much sucks at dogwalking, even though these days it's basically her job.

Attendance is over. Mr. Hubley is typing on his computer now, so the room starts getting noisy again.

"Honk-Schwee," whispers Brody from across the aisle. "Wake up, Marigold. Don't press that snooze alarm."

"Shut up, Brody," Jada tells him. "Like *you* never made an honest mistake before." She smiles sweetly at me.

"Hey, at least I remember to get dressed."

"Marigold didn't *forget to get dressed*. She thought—"

"That we all wanted to see her sexy lingerie?"

Layla snorts loudly. "Save me," she mutters, then rests her head on her arms.

I see Megan whisper something to Ashley, who laughs and turns around to stare at Layla. Then she says something to a dark-haired boy named Ethan, who'd be seriously cute if it weren't for the fact that he's Brody's best friend.

Brody makes a chimp face. *"Aah-aah, ooh-ooh, eee-eee,"* he says practically in my ear. "Got any bananas, Marigold?"

Jada rolls her eyes at me. Before I can thank her for rolling her eyes, the PA comes on. You can hear an office lady tap in the mic, then say, "Marigold Bailey? Please come to the main office immediately!"

Everyone looks at me, like *Whoa. So now you're in trouble? This is getting good.*

"Your *mother* is here," the office lady explains. "Marigold Bailey? Main office!"

"Don't wanna be late, Bananas," Brody teases. He scratches his armpits at me.

Layla makes that snorting sound again. "Evolve, Brody," she says, stretching her legs in front of her. That's when I notice the pointy-toe black leather boots she's wearing.

For a second I freeze. She looks right at me and yawns.

"You'd better go," she says, like it's permission.

I grab my backpack and skid out of the room. When I get home, I am totally tossing these slippers, I promise myself. In the same trash can as these stupid pajamas.

Inside the main office, there's my mom in her purple Wagley College sweats, her cheeks glowing, her too-long brown hair looking frizzy and wild, as if she's just run all the way over here with a bunch of tangled-up dogs. Which she probably has.

I'm so relieved to see her that I give her a huge hug even though the office ladies are staring at both of us. "Where are they?"

"Where's who? You mean the dogs?"

"I mean my clothes."

She cocks her head. "Mari, I told you. I wasn't home when you called—"

I pull her out into the hall. "Mom. Mom. You didn't bring any *clothes*?"

"How could I, baby? You were in such a big rush for me to get here! I didn't have time to go home first."

I open my mouth. Then I close it. Then I say, "So why did you even come?"

"You wanted to change out of your pj's, right? So just wear my sweats for the day. I don't mind. It's the least I can do for messing up."

"Mom," I say.

Dogs are barking off in the distance somewhere, but she doesn't seem to notice. She's grinning at me as if she's starting to enjoy this. "Is there a bathroom nearby where we can switch? I thought I remembered one from Orientation."

"Mom."

"It'll just take a second. No one will even notice."

"*Mom*. I'm *not* wearing your sweats, okay? And you're *not* going home in my pj's."

She laughs. "Why not?"

"Because you'll get arrested. For weirdness." The image of my wild-haired mother walking five dogs all over town IN MY MONKEY PAJAMAS isn't something I can bear to think about. And if she can't see for herself how impossible that would be to live down, even if we stayed in this town for another seventy-five years, then what's the point of standing in the hallway trying to explain it?

"Oh, Marigold," she says, laughing. "This is what I do; I'm *supposed* to get noticed. Think of it as free publicity."

"Right. The terrible kind."

"There *is* no terrible kind. Haven't I taught you anything by now? Take my sweats."

"No. Just . . . no."

Suddenly Mr. Shamsky, the principal, comes bursting out of the main office. "Mrs. Bailey?"

"*Ms*. But please just call me Becca."

"Are those your dogs out there?"

"Not really. I mean they're not mine technically. I'm actually just walking them."

"But you tied them to the flagpole?"

Mom's eyes flash; she looks mythological. "My daughter," she announces, "was having an emergency. So I couldn't stop to make alternative arrangements for five dogs."

He squints at my pajamas. "Everything okay now?"

"Oh, sure," I mutter.

"Great," he says, like he doesn't believe either of us. "You know, Marigold, the school nurse keeps spare clothes in her office. Just in case."

"In case of what?" Mom asks innocently.

The end-of-homeroom bell rings. I peek at Mr. Shamsky, whose shiny bald skull is turning pink.

"In case of what?" Mom repeats, louder this time.

Is she kidding? There's totally no way she doesn't get this.

She looks at me with a mischievous sparkle in her eye. And the corners of her lips are twitching, like she's trying not to smile.

Oh. Okay. I get it now. She's trying to make Mr. Shamsky say something he doesn't want to say: *IN CASE A GIRL GETS HER PERIOD*. It's one of Mom's spontaneous performances, only this time it's happening *in my school*. And in front of a live audience, because now doors are opening and kids are pouring into the hall. In fact, way off in the distance I can see Mr. Hubley, and now Jada, Ashley, and Megan are walking this way. And also Layla. And also Brody and Ethan.

"Mom," I beg her. *"Please."*

She blinks at me, disappointed.

Mr. Shamsky pretends to cough. "So anyway, Marigold, you're welcome to stop by the infirmary and check out the closet. But right now, Ms. Bailey, you need to remove those dogs. First period is starting and we can't have all this barking."

"Oh, no problem," Mom says cheerfully.

She puts her hands on my shoulders. She looks deep, deep, deep into my eyes, as if he's not even there. As if dogs aren't barking and kids aren't staring, and she's trying to locate a tiny little speck on the back of my brain. "Last chance, baby. Do you want to switch or not?"

"Not."

"Ms. Bailey," Mr. Shamsky warns.

"Okay, listen, Marigold," she says in my ear. "If I go home now and get your clothes, I could be back here in forty-five minutes. An hour tops."

"No, thanks," I say, pulling away. "I'm going to the nurse. Just go take care of the dogs now, okay?"

Then I skid down the hall, the late bell ringing in my ears.

Marbles

When I get home that afternoon, Mom is in the living room. She's in her yoga pants, upside down, surrounded by marbles.

For her this is normal.

Of course, her definition of "normal" also includes inviting a bunch of people over at three a.m. to videotape her sleeping.

And sitting onstage with a huge gooey chocolate cake, which she either eats or doesn't eat, depending on her willpower.

And wrapping herself in Saran Wrap for a piece called *Plastic Surgery*.

Oh, and pitching a tent in the park while she reads *Hamlet* in the voices of the Simpsons.

Not to mention turning herself into an electronic billboard with LEDs running all over her body to "broadcast" this poem she wrote called "LICE." She says it's about "how our overreliance on chemicals causes Mother Nature to rebel," but I think most people in the audience probably just think she's infested with electronic bugs.

Okay, I'll stop. But before you decide she's certifiable, let me explain: Mom is what is known in the biz as a performance artist. That's another way of saying she does embarrassing things in public. Sometimes she makes her audience buy tickets to watch her do those embarrassing things, but her shows are not exactly standing-room-only. So she gets these other jobs running workshops, teaching theater improvisation mostly to college students. Also walking other people's dogs. Not very well.

"Yikes, Mari. What are you wearing?" Mom says. She carefully flips herself over and lands her bare feet on the marble-covered rug. She's so good at landing that only a few marbles go rolling. Her goal is none, not one marble rolling, which I'm pretty sure ignores the law of physics.

Now she's looking at me and grinning. "Sorry, baby,

but those pants are so seventies. And that top looks like it has a disease."

"It's polka dots."

"They're pink. You look like you have chicken pox."

"Yeah, well, it's all the nurse had."

"Figures. You should have taken my sweats. Or let me go home to get you something decent." She starts picking up the marbles and plunking them one by one into an old shoebox. "So how was school?"

"The usual. Once I changed."

"Anybody give you grief?"

"Not really." Unless you count Jada telling me how she felt *so, so sorry* that I was stuck wearing such a dorky outfit. And Brody snoring in my ear and calling me Bananas all day. And Layla smirking. And staring. "The nurse says we have to wash these in hot water and bring them back tomorrow."

"Tomorrow? You mean someone's actually waiting for them?"

"I don't know. That's just what she said. I'm supposed to return them before homeroom."

She sighs. "Well, I'm happy to wash them."

"Thanks."

"Just not by tomorrow."

"Why not?" I say.

"Because, precious daughter, laundry is not my number one priority. I've got to prepare something spectacular for my workshop tomorrow, I've got this grant proposal to e-mail out by tonight, and then, of course, there's Evening Walkers." She springs up from the floor in one motion. My mother is all muscle, like the human heart.

Now she's looking out the window. "Uh-oh," she says. "It's starting to snow."

I decide to argue, just for the sheer sport of it. "What's wrong with snow? I think it looks pretty."

"That's because you don't have to schlep eight blocks to pick up greyhounds." She sighs again. "And they'll be murder to walk tonight if the sidewalks are icy. The younger one is a real squirrel-chaser and the older one has an arthritic hip. She's a sweetheart, though; her name is Mabel."

"Mom," I say loudly. "What if I went to the Laundromat myself?"

"Now? You mean in the snow?"

I shrug. "I don't mind."

"Whew, this nurse lady really has your number. Don't let her terrorize you, Mari."

"She isn't," I insist. But for Mom the conversation is already over; by now she's in the kitchenette fixing herself some ginger tea. She says it helps her digestion, but if you ask me, if there's anything wrong with her digestion, it's because she's upside down half the time.

I go to the bedroom I share with my eight-year-old sister, Kennedy. Don't laugh, okay? Yes, her name is Kennedy. My mom named her babies after a flower most people think is a weed, and a dead president. And my dad . . . well, let's just say he stopped arguing with Mom a long time ago.

Kennedy is sitting on her bed, doing what she basically always does, which is reading. She wears these geeky-cute wire-frame glasses that slip down her little upturned nose. Her other really cute feature is the space between her two front teeth, even though according to her, it makes her look stupid. Other than those things—the glasses, the nose, and the tooth-space—we look pretty similar: longish, wavy medium-brown hair parted in the middle, olive skin, dark eyes.

She notices me and closes her book. "Oh, Mari. Are you okay?"

"Why wouldn't I be?"

"Mom told me about the pj's. She feels terrible."

"No, she doesn't. She thinks it's funny. What book is that?"

She holds it up for me: *Louisa's Triumph*. It's one of those American Dreams books Kennedy is obsessed with. For a long time last year she wanted to be Jessamine the Prairie Girl, and she went around wearing braids and long flowery skirts and saying things like *Sakes alive* and *I reckon*. It drove me crazy, but Mom totally went along with it. She even made Kennedy a Jessamine rag doll, and once for a whole weekend turned our living room into a log cabin by taping brown paper bags to the walls. But then the landlord found out about it and made us take it all down because he said it was a fire hazard.

For a second I just sit on my bed, careful not to smush this patchwork Thing I'm making. (It's not a quilt; that would be way too Jessamine. Besides, the scraps are kind of random, and it's not even a rectangle. In fact, it's not even really a *shape*.) Then I take off my chicken-pox shirt and the seventies pants, and put on my Wile E. Coyote T-shirt and my favorite jeans. This is the highlight of my day, I think: getting dressed in my own clothes.

Kennedy watches. She sucks in her cheeks and

makes a fish-mouth. "Did people make fun of you?" she asks.

"Some. A little. But I was fine."

"And they made you change?"

"They didn't make me. I wanted to."

"You wanted to wear that ugly outfit?"

"Of course not. It was just the best I could do under the circumstances."

She furrows her brow. Then another fish-mouth. "Do you hate your school?"

"Not really. It's just school."

"Do you hate Mom?"

"*Kennie*. How can you ask that?"

"I didn't mean it."

"Well, then you shouldn't ask it. Because I don't."

"I take it back." She rests her chin on her knees. "And you're calling Emma?"

"What?" I say.

"She called before. First Gram called and said she was mailing us cookies, and also she had some more scraps for you, and then Emma called."

I stare at my little sister. "*When?*"

"Like, twenty minutes ago. Mom answered the phone."

23

"She did? Why didn't she tell me just now?"

Kennedy shrugs. "Don't be mad at her, Mari. She has ever so much on her mind."

I run to the kitchenette. Mom is at the table sipping her ginger tea and typing on her laptop. PROPOSAL FOR PERFORMANCE PIECE, the screen says, all the *P*'s in this jumpy-looking computer font. Beside the stove Beezer the one-eared beagle is snoozing in his metal crate. He's been here for about a week now, and I'm starting to think his owner has forgotten him.

"So Emma called?" I ask before I can catch my breath.

"Emma?" Mom acts like she's trying to remember some trivial battle from ancient history. Then her face freezes. "Oh, yes! Yikes! I completely forgot to tell you!"

"You *forgot*? Kennie said she called a few minutes ago!"

"She did. I'm really sorry! It just flew out of my mind."

I don't even know what to say to that. My mouth hangs open.

"I'm *sorry*, Marigold," Mom repeats. She waits. Then she smiles brightly. "Now you're supposed to say, *That's okay, Beloved Mother, I see how you're swamped with work, plus we're still getting settled in a brand-new town and everything is crazy, so of course I totally forgive you—*"

I shake my head.

"No? Not a good line? Yeah, you're probably right." She sits back in her chair, crosses her arms, and sighs. "Okay, Mari, look. I know you're furious at me about the Pajama Day thing. I understand; I'm mad at me too. I should have read that info packet more carefully, and you're right, I owe you a huge apology."

"Mom."

"But you know what, baby? You could have read it too. I didn't want to say that when I came to school this morning, because you were obviously so upset. But it's the truth. You're a big girl, and you should take some responsibility here. It's not all my fault."

"Mom," I say in a tight voice. "This is not about Pajama Day."

"It's not?" She sips her tea.

"You know exactly what it's about," I say, and dial Emma's number.

How It Is

"Emma?"

"*Mari?* Omigod. Is it really *you*?"

"It's really, really me."

"I can't believe it! I miss you soooo much!"

"I miss you, too." I can hear my voice cracking, but I'm happy. No, better than happy: I feel like a dusty, thirsty houseplant that's finally getting watered. Because I'm talking to my absolute best friend in the universe for the first time since we left Aldentown last month. We've been sending each other e-mails and cards and everything, but it's just not the same as an *actual conversation*.

"So what's it like?" she's asking.

"You mean Lawson?" I look out the kitchenette window. "Well, right now it's snowing."

"It's snowing here, too! God, Mari, remember last winter when we made that incredible snow fort? And then had that humongous snowball fight with Will and Matt?"

Will is her crush. Matt is mine. Was mine. There's no point in having a crush if you can't see the crushee anymore.

"And then after that we all came over here and Mom made hot chocolate and we played my brother's Wii? And you *owned* Matt on SuperSmash; you were amazing, Mari. God, it feels like two days ago."

Not to me, but I don't correct her. "So what's going on with Will, anyway?"

She tells me all about this cool-sounding after-school club they co-invented: Japanese Anime. Mostly I just listen to her talk. I can't believe how great it feels to hear her slightly-too-loud voice that always sounds as if there's a laugh inside, waiting to burst out. Maybe, I think, we can get Webcams or something, so we could actually talk face-to-face.

Finally she orders me to stop listening and say something back.

"There's not much to say," I tell her.

"Oh, Mari, come on. Have you made any friends yet?"

"Sort of." Actually, at lunch today I'd sat down with Quinn, but the whole time she kept looking over her shoulder, like she thought someone would snatch her food. And then Brody sat down and started making comments about my polka dots, so I couldn't even ask what she was so nervous about.

"You will," Emma says confidently. "Just try to open up a little, so they'll see how great you are. Are there any cute boys?"

I think about Ethan, with his dark, wavy hair. And his apelike best friend. "Not really."

"Too bad. Well, keep looking; one's bound to turn up." She pauses. "So anyway. What's your polish status?"

I study my fingernails. Not only are they totally unpolished, they're also chipped and dirty. The truth is, ever since the move, I haven't even thought about them. "Um, right now I'm wearing Fun in the Sun."

"Oh, I *love* that color!" she squeals. "That's the one with, what was it? Oh, yes. Pearly undertones."

I grin. "And a hint of opalescence."

"And a whiff of springtime."

"And romantic evenings before the fire. And Paris in the rain."

"Ooh la la. Oh, but wait. How can Fun in the Sun mean Paris in the *rain*?"

"It's a sun shower," I say. "With a gorgeous rainbow at the end."

She laughs. I love her laugh. Then she says, "God, it's just so awful that we can't hang out anymore."

"I know."

"And so unfair! It's not like *we* messed up."

I tear off a ragged bit of pinky-nail. "Yeah. We didn't."

She sighs. "Well. No use going into all that again, I guess. So tell me something else about your brand-new life. Tell me about school."

"You really want to hear that?"

"Of course I do!" she swears, so I tell her about the whole Pajama Day ordeal.

"That's *horrible*," she says. "Did your mom at least apologize?"

"Sort of. She said she was mad at herself, but that it was my fault too."

"Really? How was it *your* fault?"

"I don't know. I could have read the school calendar."

"Could you have?"

It takes Emma's question to focus my brain on the fact that yes, okay, I actually *could* have read the dumb calendar. I mean, Mom did tear up the New Student Info Packet for Beezer's crate-bed, but first it had been sitting for, like, a week on the kitchenette counter with all the bills and junk mail. So technically yes, I could have read it myself. And with Mom's organizational track record, I probably should have.

Before I can admit this, though, Emma's mom starts yelling. I can't hear exactly what she's saying, but I can make out enough of the tone to know that Trisha Hartley wants her daughter off the phone. This minute.

"Look, gotta go," Emma says quickly.

"Your mom?"

"Yeah." She laughs awkwardly. "You know how it is."

"Has she . . . you know. Said anything?"

"Not specifically. But I'm still thinking that if we give it enough time, she'll calm down. And then maybe you can visit in the summer."

I swallow. "That would be so great, Em."

"EMMA," I hear. *"WHAT DID I JUST SAY? DO YOU THINK I'M DEAF? DO YOU THINK I DON'T KNOW WHO YOU'RE TALKING TO?"*

"See you online," she whispers. And then she hangs up.

Terrible Manners

When I was a little kid, I thought my mom was the coolest mother in existence. No, I *knew* she was. Because everybody said so.

I remember one time in second grade when all the parents were supposed to come to our classroom and talk about their jobs. Matt's mom went first and talked about how she was a dermatologist, and how you should always wear sunscreen. Will's mom talked about working in a bank. Emma's dad talked about marketing, only it was so boring I didn't listen.

And then Mom walked to the front of the classroom.

And started taking off her clothes.

Everyone gasped. Until they realized that under her clothes was a scuba-diving outfit. Which was cool all by itself, really.

But then she reached into a giant tote bag she'd brought, and took out three beach towels, which she carefully spread on the floor. She placed a chair on the beach towels and sat down. Then she grinned at the class and held up a giant bottle of imported olive oil. She twisted off the cap slowly, and before anyone could stop her, she poured some of it into her mouth.

"Eww," said the class.

Except she didn't just drink it. She also poured it all over her scuba-diving outfit. In her lap, down her chest, even on her arms and legs. She also poured some of it onto her hair, and let it drip down her face. She was so oily and shiny under the fluorescent classroom lights that she practically glowed.

At first no one knew what to say. "What's your job?" a kid named Bradley Miller called out. "Are you a weirdo?"

Mom shook her head. Oil spattered on the towels.

"Eww," said the class again, louder this time.

"Are you a grease monster?" Sean Koplik asked, laughing so hard he fell out of his chair. "Are you a french fry?"

"Nope," Mom said.

"Are you a weirdo?" Bradley repeated.

"Ms. Bailey?" Our second-grade teacher, Mr. O'Neill, was young and fun, but he was definitely getting a little nervous. "Can you please give us a clue about your profession? We're kind of stumped here."

Mom grinned. "I'm the United States."

The class stared.

"I'm guzzling oil," she explained. "And making a big mess. Isn't that silly?"

The class roared. I mean, if you want to get a whole bunch of seven-year-olds to instantly fall in love with you, Mom had the secret formula. They clapped and jumped out of their seats and begged her to keep pouring oil over her head, but finally she wiped herself off with some paper towels and explained that she was sort of an artist, but not the easel type. She did performance art, she explained, using her body to make you see boring, everyday things in a surprising new way. "And possibly even think a little," she added. Oh, and she was doing a one-woman show this weekend at the community theater, so if the class wanted to see more, they should tell their parents to buy tickets.

"Thanks, Ms. Bailey," Mr. O'Neill said, smiling. "That was certainly memorable."

And it was. The kids all remembered to tell their parents, and that Saturday, Mom had maybe her best turnout ever. I forget what she did onstage—I think it was *Plastic Surgery*—but whatever it was, it didn't go over as well as *Guzzling Oil*. Which the kids in my class couldn't stop talking about, constantly asking me if my mom wore a scuba suit at home, and if the floors in our apartment were all slippery. Finally somebody's mom—I think it was Sean Koplik's—complained to the principal that she caught her kid drinking canola, so the principal called Mom and accused her of "sending the wrong message."

"Excuse me," Mom shouted into the receiver. "But under the First Amendment of the Constitution I have *every right* to speak out about protecting our planet. And maybe if you folks were teaching energy awareness and global responsibility, my daughter would actually be learning something *important*!"

I couldn't hear the rest of the conversation, but from the way Mom slammed her bedroom door afterward, I could tell she was really upset. And that night at dinner, Mom didn't eat very much. Or talk very much either.

Finally she said, "I think I may have blown it with your principal, Mari."

"It's okay," I told her. "Nobody likes him, anyway."

"That's not the point." She sighed. "I just don't want him taking it out on you."

"But he never even yells at me."

"Really? Well, let's keep it that way. *No youthful hijinks, all right, young lady?*" She wagged her finger, like she was scolding me. And then all of a sudden she grinned, like the whole thing was a joke.

But it wasn't. Because the next thing I knew, Mom got uninvited from chaperoning the second-grade trip to the planetarium, and four kids in the class told me their parents wouldn't let them come to my house anymore.

"Your mom's a weirdo," Bradley Miller said to me at recess one day.

"No, she's not, she's an artist," I'd answered loudly. Kids were starting to crowd around, so I added, "And if she's so weird, how come you clapped for her? How come you came to the theater afterward?"

"Because she's funny," Bradley said. "But now everyone thinks she's nuts."

"And she also had a big fight with the principal,"

said this older girl I didn't even know. Which was how I knew that word had gotten out, and it was all over school now, probably all over town.

Right around this time, the theater told Mom it was canceling her show. (Mom threatened to perform for free in the small park across the street from the theater; they said, "Go ahead," so she did, wrapping herself with Saran Wrap for all the nannies and the pigeons.) The next year, Mom lost her job teaching improv at the community college. By the time I was in fourth grade, she started walking dogs to pay the rent.

We moved in the middle of sixth grade, the second year of middle school. At the time Mom said it was so that we could live closer to Dad, but they'd been divorced since I was in first grade, and not together very much before that, so I had my doubts. He was renting a small house about three miles from our new apartment building, but he was a magazine photographer always off "on assignment," so he was practically never there. I don't know if Mom had totally realized this before we'd moved. Maybe she expected us to become one big happy divorced family. Or maybe she thought if he saw us more often, he'd pay for more stuff; I know around then she was pretty worried about money.

Anyway, the whole time we were setting up the new apartment, she was in a great mood. She even unpacked an old scrapbook of Dad's photos, and showed Kennedy and me a bunch of landscape shots he'd taken during his study-abroad year in India. I thought they were pretty amazing, but I could see by the slow, dreamy way Mom turned the scrapbook pages that they meant something else to her. Then she gave us a big speech about what a brilliant photographer he was, how daring and original, how proud she was that he'd dedicated his life to his art.

"You do that too," I reminded her. "Dedicate your life to your art."

"You think so?" she answered. "Because *I* think I dedicate my life to my two precious daughters." She kissed my cheek and then Kennedy's, closed the scrapbook, and stuck it in her nightstand.

We'd been living in the new apartment for about a week when one day, right after Easter, Dad called. He'd be in town for the next month or so, he said, and wanted to invite Kennedy and me over "for Sunday dinner." This was surprising, because whenever we saw Dad, he always drove to our place and took us out for "ethnic food," which usually meant Chinese. And then afterward we'd do mini golf or go to a movie, anything where we wouldn't have to talk very much.

But now he was inviting us "for Sunday dinner," as if it were a sacred Bailey family ritual. Kennedy was so excited she actually put on a prairie dress, and I decided to wear my jean skirt—dressier than my usual jeans, but not too hyper-formal. Mom hugged us and told us we both looked gorgeous, and then she dropped us off in the driveway of Dad's small red house.

This short, perky woman with streaky highlights and a fake-looking bronzer tan answered the door. When Kennedy and I stood there like maybe we'd gotten the address wrong, Dad came rushing over to introduce her as Mona. And then he casually mentioned that she was a "family friend."

"Whose family?" I asked. Dad gave me a look that meant: *Don't start being difficult, Marigold. I've been divorced for five years, and I'm allowed to have girlfriends. And I will NOT allow you to mess this up for me.*

So, of course, I stopped looking at him.

Things went downhill from there. For dinner Mona made baby back ribs, not knowing that Kennedy had just turned vegetarian, and that serving anything with the word "baby" in the title was just the sort of thing that would make my sister totally lose it. By lose it I mean burst into tears and not be able to stop sniffling, even though Mona kept handing her paper napkins and saying things like, "Honey, the animal is already dead."

"Um, Mona? That's kind of the point," I informed her, purposely avoiding Dad's eyes.

Finally Dad cleared off the table and ordered an olive pizza for Kennedy, and we all watched pro wrestling on TV until none of us could stand it anymore. Then he drove Kennedy and me back to our apartment.

"Maybe next time we'll go bowling," Dad said as we got out of the car.

"Uh-huh," Kennedy said cheerfully. "Well, see you!" She ran into our apartment building as if she was trying to get out of a rainstorm.

"Bye, Dad," I said. I suddenly felt sorry that we'd both given him such a hard time. So I leaned into the car and kissed his cheek.

"Bye, Monster," he said sadly. "I'm sorry it was such a bad evening."

"It wasn't so bad," I lied. "Tell Mona thanks for the dinner."

"I will. She'll be glad you said that." He reached for

my hand and squeezed it. Then he looked into my eyes. "Everything okay at home?"

"Sure. Why wouldn't it be?"

He kept holding my hand. "I mean with Mom."

"She's great," I said enthusiastically. "Busy with the dogs. She's starting a drama club at the Y and learning sign language for this new piece she's working on."

"Wow, sign language." He shook his head. "Your mom's really something."

"Oh, I know."

He opened his hand slowly, as if he didn't want to let go. "Well, call me if you need anything, okay, Monster? Kennie, too."

"We will. Bye, Dad!"

"Love you."

"Love you, too!" I blew him another kiss and ran inside.

By the time I reached our apartment, Kennedy had blabbed to Mom all about Mona, and Mom was calling Dad's cell to give a loud screaming speech about Sensitivity and Respecting Your Daughters' Choices and Putting Your Family First. (One thing about performance artists: They know how to get attention.) The landlord banged on our front door and told Mom that he was sick of all the noise, and that if she didn't shut up, and also stop dropping marbles on the floor and bringing barking dogs up and down the stairs, he'd raise the rent. "GO AHEAD!" she yelled back at him. "I DARE YOU."

So he did.

About a month later Mom informed us that we'd be moving to Aldentown, where two old friends of hers named Beau and Bobbi were opening the Two Beez Performing Arts Café. Aldentown would be perfect for us, Mom said. She'd appear at the Café every other Saturday night, and Beau and Bobbi had some friends at the local college who would see if Mom could run a workshop. We wouldn't be living too far away from Gram, and we could visit Dad when he was in town. "If you really *want* to," she added.

"Of course we do," I said, shocked that this was even a question.

She snorted. "What about The Horrible Mona Woman?" That was her name for Mona; she was using it all the time now.

"She's really not so horrible, Mom."

Mom's eyes got big. "How can you say that, Mari? After the insensitive way she treated Kennedy? Serving her *baby meat*?"

"It wasn't Mona's fault."

"Oh, so you're sticking up for her?"

"No. But how was she supposed to know Kennie was a vegetarian? Even Dad didn't know." I paused. "How come? Didn't you tell him?"

"Of course I did! You think I'd purposely not tell him something so important? I'm such a terrible mother? And besides," she said, tossing books into a cardboard packing box, "you girls are always talking to him on the phone. I'm sure Kennie just told him herself."

"Then how come he didn't know?" For a second I considered shutting up, like I usually did. But this time, for some crazy reason, I kept going. "You know what I think, Mom? I think Dad has a serious girlfriend and you're jealous. So you're kind of overdramatizing."

"I'm *what*?" Mom said. Her olive-colored skin—the skin we all three have, Mom, Kennedy, and me—looked weirdly pale, as if I were looking at her through tracing paper.

"Mona isn't evil," I said. "You shouldn't turn her into some kind of stage character. Or performance topic."

"Mari. I can't believe you're talking to me like this. How can you possibly accuse me—"

"She's just this *person*. She didn't mean to hurt

anybody; she was just trying to be nice. And I feel bad I was so snarky to her."

"You were snarky?"

I nodded.

"What did you do?"

"I was rude when she tried to calm down Kennie. And I didn't thank her for making dinner."

Mom blinked. "That's *terrible manners*," she scolded.

All of a sudden we both started giggling. Not specifically about The Horrible Mona Woman or Dad. Who knows what we were laughing about, actually. Maybe nothing.

That night Mom took Kennedy and me to the movies. I don't remember very much about it, except that Mom called it a "chick flick" and said it was "just what the doctor ordered." ("Is somebody sick?" Kennedy asked worriedly, and Mom just laughed and kissed her on the nose.) For dinner we ate chocolate—boxes of Milk Duds and Raisinets and a big bag of Tootsie Rolls. But we weren't messy; we threw away every bit of our trash. Mom had spent too many hours in theaters to let us be disrespectful of the cleanup crew, she said.

Chocolate Night

We moved to Aldentown with only three weeks left to the school year. Most parents would have waited until summer vacation, I knew, but Mom had insisted that Beau and Bobbi were counting on her to perform, and that we had to get to Aldentown as soon as we possibly could. And then of course once we got there, and all the boxes had been re-unpacked, she insisted that Kennedy and I start school the following Monday to "get into the swing of things."

"Can't we just wait until September?" I begged her. I was convinced that the least she owed us was the chance to start school with everybody else. Plus I was just fine hanging out in my tiny new bedroom, talking with Kennedy, working on my patchwork Thing. Right before we moved, Gram had mailed me a big box of scraps, and I guess it kind of comforted me to be stitching them together. I liked designing patterns with the weird, clashing fabric, and also making something that kept changing shape. But mostly what I think I liked was the soothing rhythm of sewing: poke, pull, poke, pull.

"No, Mari, you can't," Mom answered me firmly. She put her hands on my shoulders and looked right into my face. "Let me tell you something, baby: Whenever I add a new dog to my Walkers, I can tell right away if it's going to work out. And you know how I know? I watch if the dog joins right in, sniffing all the other dogs' butts, or if he hangs back, like he's afraid. The ones who hang back always tangle the leashes."

I rolled my eyes. "Oh, great. You're comparing me to a dog?"

She threw her head back and laughed. "I mean it as the highest compliment. Get in there and sniff everyone's butt, Marigold."

Another thing about my mom: She knows how to make a point.

So I started Aldentown Middle at the end of May, the time of year when everybody is sick of school, and also sick of everybody else, and fights break out. But it didn't take a whole lot of butt-sniffing to figure out that at this school, the sixth grade wasn't just fighting. It was at war.

For some reason nobody seemed to know, Sarah Wong and Ally Ferrara, the two most powerful girls in the grade, had decided that they were mortal enemies, and that everyone had to choose sides. You had two choices at lunch: You could sit at Ally's table or at Sarah's table, and once you made your choice, that was it.

Of course, if I was the kind of join-right-in dog Mom approved of, I'd have immediately walked right up to these girls, and decided who would make the better friend, or at least the worse enemy. But I'm a leash-tangler. I admit it. In most new situations, I hang back, take my time, try to figure out what I'm thinking. And feeling. Anyway, my point is, I wasn't going to show up at Aldentown Middle School and make a whole bunch of quick decisions about people, especially when those decisions were the kind you couldn't unmake. So I kept to myself in the lunchroom, painting cream-cheese pictures on a rubbery bagel. I was fine like this for three straight lunches. And then on the fourth lunch, I realized that Emma Hartley had slid into the seat beside me.

Right away I could tell she was hiding. This shocked me. I mean, I'd been in school less than a week, but already I'd noticed how popular she was. And not just popular: athletic, fashionable, smiley. Girls like this usually totally psyched me out, and I didn't even *try* to get to know them. But there was something about the way Emma was sitting there, scraping the crust off her sandwich with grape-colored fingernails, that made me ask if she was okay.

She looked up at me. Her light brown eyes almost matched her auburn hair. "No," she said, a little too loudly. "I *hate* all this fighting."

"You mean between Ally and Sarah?"

She nodded. "It's not even *about* anything. And I've always been friends with both of them, so how can I possibly choose sides?"

"Yeah," I said, "it's so much easier when there's a villain." I'd been thinking about this a lot lately, how Mom loved it when she had something—or someone—to make her angry. It wasn't even just that it gave her material for her art. It's like it gave her energy.

Emma smiled at that. "Your name is Marigold, right? That's so funny; I just bought some nail polish called Marigold."

"You did?" I laughed. "Was it orange?"

"Sort of a yellow-orange. I thought it would be fun and summery, kind of a different look, but on me it didn't work. Can I give it to you?"

"Sure," I said excitedly, even though I never wore nail polish.

"I have soccer practice this afternoon. Are you free tomorrow?"

Of course I was; I'd just moved in, so it wasn't like I had a whole bunch of after-school clubs or dentist appointments all lined up.

And so, amazingly, starting the very next day, Emma and I began spending practically all her soccer-free afternoons together. We didn't do anything special, mostly just listening to music, encouraging each other's crushes, polishing our fingernails. I was the official polisher; Emma's nails came out blobby and tacky if she did them herself, and I liked being careful, so I always did us both. We'd go to Rite Aid after school and pick out the colors with the best names *(Hot Date! Puppy Love! Cotton Candy! Sugar Rush!)*. She'd pay for the polish with her allowance money, and never ask me to pay her back. And usually we'd end up at my apartment, where we'd watch MTV or old episodes of *The Simpsons*, and apply three glossy coats, first to her nails, then to mine.

The other main thing we did was complain about our moms. In fact, the more I got to know Emma, the more I told her about Mom's performances, and the dogwalking, and the moving, and the marbles. Once I even told her I wished I could switch places with her, and live in a big, soap-smelling house with a dad whose life wasn't Dedicated to Art, and a mom who knew everybody in town and didn't yell at principals and pour oil all over her head.

"Listen, Mari," Emma said to me. "You *think* your mom's harder to live with than mine, but she's not. I mean, okay, so maybe she drives you crazy in public"— this was about the time Mom had taken up unicycling on the school soccer fields to improve her balance— "but at least she doesn't nag you about lining up your sneakers at a one-hundred-and-eighty-degree angle to your bed. And I bet she doesn't go ballistic if there's a leftover hair in your hairbrush."

"Wait," I said, laughing. "Stop. Your mom cares if there's a single hair in your hairbrush?"

Emma shook a bottle of Pink-tastic so hard I could hear the little brush rattling inside. Then she twisted off the lid and handed it to me.

"I'm not exaggerating," she insisted. "And she won't let up until the hair is gone. *Emma, have you taken care of the situation? It's been three minutes since my last reminder. Do I really have to jump up and down and turn purple again?* I'm serious, Mari. My mom's obsessed. She never relaxes about *anything*."

"Whoa," I said, slowly and neatly brushing the Pink-tastic on Emma's ragged thumbnails.

"And does she go after my brothers like that? Even though all four of them are total slobs? No. She cleans up after them. You know why?" She blew on her thumbs. "Because they're boys."

"That's so unfair!"

"Tell me about it." A very sweet mutt that Mom was babysitting named Maxie came over and licked Emma on the nose. She laughed. "Just be thankful for what you've got."

"Oh, I am," I admitted. "I was just kidding about switching places." And then I scratched Maxie between the ears, which wasn't easy to do with my own sticky nails.

That was during the summer. By the fall of seventh grade, Emma was getting so frustrated with her mom's constant nagging that she started eating dinner with us every Friday night, and sometimes during the week, too, when she didn't have soccer practice. Mrs. Hartley wasn't too sure about Mom—I could tell this by her eyebrow angle and her no-teeth smile when she asked polite questions about Mom's "stage act." But she had four sons who did a million team sports each, and I think she was glad sometimes that she didn't have to rush home from whatever practice to fix dinner for Emma. So she always let Emma stay at our apartment, even though, from Emma's side of the phone conversation, you could tell her mom was starting to put up some sort of argument.

One Friday evening in early November, Emma and I were sitting in the living room waiting for our nails (that day, Juicy Passionfruit) to dry. Suddenly Mom walked in the front door and immediately flopped on the sofa next to Emma.

"Well, girls, I give up," she announced.

"You give what up?" I asked.

"The whole performance thing," Mom said. "All of it."

I sighed. I'd heard this one before. "What happened?"

"What do you *think* happened, Mari? They rejected my grant proposal."

"Who did?" Emma asked, outraged.

"The American Arts Council."

Emma squinted at me like *Who? What? How dare they?*

I examined a passionfruit-colored pinky nail. "Did they say why this time?"

"No," Mom said. "My guess, and this is based on pure speculation, is that they think paintball is more of a *sport* than an *artistic medium*. And they think 'random' is a curse word. Just my theory, of course."

"Maybe you can get the money for your show somewhere else," Emma suggested.

"Hmmph," Mom said. She put up her feet on the coffee table. She twirled her wild frizzy hair into a ponytail, then let it sproing out angrily. "What money? What show? Mari, I hate to say it, but this looks like a definite Chocolate Night."

Emma's eyes lit up. "A what?"

"Chocolate Night," I said. "It's sort of a family tradition. It's what we save for those special sucky moments."

Mom poked my arm. "Like the time my beloved daughter took sides with The Horrible Mona Woman."

"Dad's girlfriend," I explained.

Mom snorted. "Or the time I rented the Lewisville Community Theater for a special performance of *Swan Lake*—"

"Mom played all the parts," I said. "On rollerblades."

"You bet," Mom said. "It was fantastic. Except for one small detail: Nobody showed up."

"Gram did. And Uncle Robby."

"Uncle Robby doesn't count, Marigold. He left before intermission."

"Yeah, well, he had to go to work. And anyway Gram loved it."

"Because she's my *mother.* She's *required* to love it." Mom stuck out her tongue at me. "So after that fiasco we had a huge feast of Snickers bars and Tootsie Rolls."

"And Kennie threw up."

"But not from the chocolate. From the excitement." Mom got up and did a yoga stretch. Downward Dog, or some semi-alarming name like that. "Anyway, Emma, the moral of the story is, you're welcome to stay for dinner. If you don't mind shameless self-indulgence."

"Why would I mind?" Emma said, laughing.

A few minutes later, Mom went back out to Stop & Shop. When she came back, she called us all to the table and passed out Dove Bars and Twizzlers and Tootsie Rolls and Milky Ways. (The Twizzlers were mainly for Kennedy, who was still a little shaken from the last Chocolate Night.) We drank gallons of milk and Emma told hilarious stories about her four slobby brothers, like the time the oldest one, named Seth, microwaved an unopened can of SpaghettiOs and almost incinerated the house. By seven thirty there were candy wrappers all over the kitchenette and we were feeling a little sick. But at least Mom was laughing along with the rest of us, which was the whole purpose of Chocolate Night.

Only then, unfortunately, Trisha Hartley showed up.

Completely Bonkers

At first Emma's mom stood there in the kitchenette looking stunned. Everything about her was so straight and perfect—her shoulder-length blond hair, her white teeth, the tiny cables on her turquoise sweater—but she had this twitchy look on her face like, *Okay, Trisha, don't panic, you can handle this.*

"Is this a birthday party?" she asked, trying to do a good-sport smile. "Is it Kennedy's?"

"Nuh-uh," said Kennedy, still chomping on a Twizzler. "My birthday's in August. I just had it three months ago."

"So then . . . it's Marigold's?"

I glanced at Mom. She shrugged like, *Hey, don't look at me.*

"Not yet," I said.

"Then yours, Rebecca?"

"Call me Becca. And no, it's not my birthday, thank you very much. I'm in no hurry for another one."

Mrs. Hartley's cheeks were getting pink. Pinker, I mean; she always wore tons of blush. "I'm sorry, I don't understand."

"Mom didn't get funding for her new performance piece," Kennedy announced. "Because they didn't like paintball. Or the word 'random.' So we're having Chocolate Night."

"Chocolate Night? You mean . . . what? Pigging out on candy?"

"Oh, come on, Mom," Emma said, pretending to laugh. "We were just trying to cheer up Mrs. Bailey."

"Becca," Mom reminded her. "I *hate* being called Mrs. Bailey."

Mrs. Hartley raised one perfectly tweezed eyebrow. "And Becca, do you eat like this often?"

"Oh no," I cut in. "We're very careful about food." Which was true, actually: For supper we usually had tons of salads and whole grain pasta and cheesy casseroles and homemade soup. I turned to Mom so she could back me up on this, but she just looked at me like, *Who is this woman, Marigold, and what's she doing in my kitchen?*

"I'm a vegetarian," Kennedy was saying proudly. "I'm always ever so careful about what I eat."

"That's wonderful, honey," Mrs. Hartley told Kennedy in this sticky-sweet voice. "And does your mommy make you real meals sometimes? With protein and fruits and vegetables—"

Mom opened her mouth, and then immediately snapped it shut.

"And do you always brush your teeth and see the dentist?" Mrs. Hartley continued.

Emma grabbed her mom's sleeve. "Let's go," she whispered. "You're starting a fight."

"What am *I* starting?" Mrs. Hartley looked amazed. "*I* haven't done anything wrong!"

"You're criticizing Becca."

"What did I say?"

"You're saying she's feeding her kids wrong. And not taking them to the dentist."

"I'm not intending to *offend* her, sweetheart. But she invites you here for supper and then offers you an entire meal of unhealthy junk—"

"We had milk," Emma said desperately.

"Milk," Mrs. Hartley repeated. "Milk is not a balanced meal."

"Well, maybe this wasn't intended to *be* a balanced meal," Mom finally exploded. "Listen, Trisha, you know why your daughter spends so much time here? It's because you're driving her completely bonkers."

Mrs. Hartley looked at Mom as if she was a squished worm on the sidewalk. "You have no right to speak to me that way. Or to feed my daughter garbage. I'm sorry you didn't get money for your stage act, but that's no reason to stop being a responsible parent."

Now Mom's eyes were enormous. "You're saying I'm not a responsible parent? And that it's because of *my art*?"

"Your art?" Mrs. Hartley actually laughed. "That's what you call it? Standing onstage making a complete fool of yourself—"

"Excuse me, Trisha, but you've never even seen me perform!"

"I don't have to. I've heard all about your performances from Emma."

"What?" Mom blinked first at Emma, then at me.

"I didn't tell her anything," I said quickly. "Just about 'LICE'—"

"And the oil," Mrs. Hartley said. "And the plastic surgery. And that cartoon business with Shakespeare."

"Mom is very sensitive about her work," Kennedy suddenly announced. Then she threw up.

Everybody rushed to Kennedy's side. She was fine, she kept saying, just too many Twizzlers. But she looked chalky white and sort of focused, like she might throw up again any minute, so Mom took her to the bathroom, and Emma dragged Mrs. Hartley out the door.

See you Monday, Emma mouthed at me. She waved her Juicy Passionfruit fingernails and tried to smile.

I tried to smile back. But I was terrified. All I could think was, *What if Mrs. Hartley won't let Emma come here anymore? What if she won't let me go to their house? What if, thanks to Mom, I lose the best friend I ever had?*

I sewed a million scraps that weekend. Poke, pull, poke, pull.

But it didn't help.

Monday finally came, and the first thing Emma and I did in homeroom was tell each other how incredibly sorry we were for our moms' behavior. We even had a pretend-argument about Whose Mom was Crazier. (I said mine, although the truth was, I'd started to think

Trisha Hartley was catching up in that contest.)

We also agreed that for the next few weeks it would be better if Emma didn't stay for supper, and that in general we should keep our mothers as far apart as possible. And that wasn't hard, because Mom had suddenly gotten an inspiration for a new performance piece. So when she wasn't dogwalking or unicycling or doing yoga in the living room, she was spending tons of time at the Two Beez Performing Arts Café, rehearsing this new character she'd invented, and getting feedback from the waiters. Our apartment was a total mess, but we didn't even mind because Mom was happy.

Two weeks later, she announced that she was ready to perform. The night before, she asked me if I wanted to invite Emma, who I knew would be thrilled at the invitation. "And Trisha might be interested too," Mom added casually.

"Mrs. Hartley?" I said slowly. "You're inviting her to your *performance*?"

"Why not?"

"Because, no offense, Mom, but I don't think she'll come."

"Oh, I bet she will," Mom answered. "She's fascinated by my 'stage act.'"

"*Fascinated?* She thinks it's stupid!"

Mom just laughed. "She'll be there, baby. You watch."

Now you're probably thinking: *Okay, Marigold. You know your mother is totally out of control, and capable of anything. So why didn't you suspect that if she was inviting Trisha Hartley, she had to have some sort of warped ulterior motive?*

Because the truth is, up to this exact point, I had no idea that my mother *was* capable of anything. I mean, I always knew she was ready to embarrass herself. And to embarrass me, too, for the Sake of Art, and all that. But always, even when she Guzzled Oil back when I was in second grade, there was a definite limit: At a certain point in her act, she'd clean herself up and explain her message. Which was usually something about The Evils of Consumerism or Eroding Constitutional Values or The Perils to Our Planet. (Although sometimes, of course, it was just Aren't I Creative? Buy Tickets to My Show.) Anyway, what you have to understand is that I was completely in the dark about Saturday night, November 30, which was the world premiere of Mom's new performance piece.

Entitled *Nu-Trisha, Mother of Doom.*

Point of View

Emma, Mrs. Hartley, Kennedy, and I were seated at a sticky little table in the back of the Two Beez Café, watching the regular bunch of Saturday performers get up in front of the mic: Joey Something, who played acoustic guitar; Amanda Somebody, who sang Carrie Underwood; some angry high school girl, who rapped about her cheating boyfriend. I wasn't sure why Mrs. Hartley had even come (Curiosity? To make sure Emma wasn't eating garbage?). But whatever the reason, she frowned when Mom stomped into the spotlight with spray-painted yellow hair, pink smears on her cheeks like warpaint, and a turquoise sweater with glow-in-the-dark cables. And as soon as Mom thundered, "GREETINGS, MORTALS. I AM NU-TRISHA, MOTHER OF DOOM," my stomach knotted up, and I thought I might literally faint.

"Just go," I whispered to Emma. "Leave *now*."

"Why?" Emma said. "She's a riot." She grinned as Mom—I mean, Nu-Trisha—smashed some veggies together and hurled them at one of our big soup pots.

"It's not going to stay funny," I insisted. "Please just trust me on this, okay?"

"Is this supposed to make sense, Marigold?" Mrs. Hartley asked. "Because I truthfully don't understand what your mom's trying to do up there."

"She's smashing vegetables," Emma whispered.

"I can see that. But is there a point?"

I breathed. Mrs. Hartley didn't get it; maybe everything would be okay. "It's just dumb. Don't feel you have to stay, Mrs. Hartley. Really, Mom totally won't mind if you guys walk out."

"But she invited us," Mrs. Hartley protested.

"Because she felt bad about Chocolate Night. And it was extremely nice of you to come tonight, but now you can both leave. *Please*."

Kennedy had been watching Mom with the same patient look she always had at these performances, but now she poked me in the ribs. "You shouldn't be talking, Mari. It distracts Mom."

"Good," I muttered. "I hope it does."

Suddenly Emma figured out what was going on. Her face got pale; I could tell even though the Two Beez was pretty dark. "Come on," she said to her mother. "Let's get out of here."

"Just leave?" Mrs. Hartley asked. You could tell she'd never walked out on anything before, and considered it Terrible Manners.

Emma stood. So then Mrs. Hartley got up too.

Sorry, I mouthed to Emma, but she didn't even look at me.

They headed quickly toward the door, Mrs. Hartley first, Emma following right behind. And then there was a loud boom. Mom was banging with a ladle on the veggie pot. It sounded like thunder.

"HALT, MORTALS. ARE YOU WALKING OUT? NOBODY WALKS OUT ON NU-TRISHA."

Ulp, I thought.

"*I* SET THE STANDARDS FOR BEHAVIOR. *I* PASS JUDGMENT ON ALL MOTHERS. *I* FIX BALANCED MEALS." She threw a tomato at the soup pot. "AND I INTEND TO OFFEND."

Mrs. Hartley froze.

Then she flew out the front door of the Two Beez Performing Arts Café, with Emma running after her.

For maybe three seconds there was total silence. Then Joey the Guitarist and the high school rapper burst out laughing. Beau and Bobbi, sitting by the kitchen, started laughing too. Even the waiters were laughing.

Not me, though. "Oh, Mom, how could you?" I cried. And I ran out the door after Emma and her mother.

But they were already gone.

I ran around the block a few times, searching for them, not knowing where to go. It was a drizzly and chilly night, but I sure didn't want to go back inside the Café, so finally, after about ten minutes, I just went home. First thing when I got back to the apartment, I called Emma's house. (Emma didn't have a cell anymore because she kept losing them, and Mrs. Hartley had decided to teach her a lesson about Personal Responsibility.) One of Emma's four slobby brothers—I think it was Seth— answered and promised to give Emma the message. So I waited. But she never called back. Then I tried calling her house again. And then again, about twenty minutes later. But both times the phone just rang and rang.

So that's how I knew that she was really, really mad. Not just at Mom, but amazingly, *at me*. Even though I hadn't known anything about Mom's performance ahead of time. Even though, as soon as I'd figured it out, I'd begged Emma to leave.

So I started to cry. Which is not something I did very often. But this was a special occasion.

I thought about calling Dad right then. He'd be the perfect person to talk to, I thought, because he totally understood about Mom. But it was a Saturday night. He was probably out somewhere with The Horrible Mona Woman, if he happened to be in town. And anyway, even if he was around to answer, he was a picture person, not a word person, and especially not a words-on-the-telephone person. So I stopped dialing his cell mid-number, and called Gram instead.

"Oh, cookie," she said as soon as she heard my voice. "What *happened*?"

"Your daughter just ruined my life," I said, bursting into tears all over again. Finally I stopped crying and told her about the Two Beez Café.

She listened, making little *tsk, tsk* sounds every once in a while, so I could tell she was still there. Then she said, "Well, Becca is a very difficult person sometimes. This is not news, Mari."

"I know!"

"She put you in a terrible spot with your friend. And there's never any excuse for humiliating anybody. Especially in public."

"I know." Gram was great.

"But it sounds to me as if your friend's mom dealt a low blow. And struck first."

"What?" I sniffled. "Anyway, so what if she did?"

"Well, nobody insults your mom's art. We may not always care for it, honey, but it's who she is."

I didn't answer.

"And nobody, I mean *nobody*, insults her as a mother. That's what she cares about more than *anything*."

I wiped my nose. "Well, if she cares about being a mother so much, why did she just wreck the best friendship I ever had?"

"Oh, Marigold. If Emma is really your best friend, she'll calm down. And she'll realize you had nothing to do with Becca's performance."

"Okay," I said doubtfully. "But what if she doesn't?"

"She will. Just give your friend some time."

"Okay." It wasn't like I had much of a choice, anyway.

"And Mari?" She paused. "Will you do something for me, cookie? Try sometimes to understand your mom's point of view."

"*Her* point of view?"

Gram laughed. "She has one, strangely enough."

By the time Mom and Kennedy got home from the Two Beez about a half hour later, Gram had called Mom on her cell, so she had some microscopic clue about what I was feeling.

"Oh, Mari, try not to overreact," she said as she scrubbed off her makeup in the bathroom. "Everyone thought Nu-Trisha was hilarious. Beau and Bobbi said it was maybe my best performance ever."

"Yeah?" I said. "Well, *Mrs. Hartley* didn't think it was funny."

"She will when she has a chance to think about it."

"You're sure about that? Positive?"

"Of course," Mom said confidently. "And she'll realize that I wasn't portraying her as a *person*. I was just creating a *character*."

I snorted.

"A type," Mom continued. "A symbol. Of smug, judgmental, narrow-minded—"

Whatever. Despite what Gram had said, I was so *not* in the mood to hear Mom's point of view that night. Because really, that was just about all I ever heard, it seemed.

I walked out of the bathroom and pretty much didn't talk to her for a solid week.

It took Emma just about that long—a solid week—to stop freaking out. She talked to me at school, of course, but she was serious and quiet, and she kept sighing a lot and saying things like, "I hate it when people are angry," and "I wish things were back to normal."

"You don't think this was my fault, right?" I asked for maybe the tenth time in five days. We were walking home from school, but this time we didn't stop at Rite Aid.

"Of course not," she answered, avoiding my eyes. "I just wish your mom—"

My throat tightened. "My mom what?"

"I don't know. Knew my mom better. She's really not so bad. When she's not incredibly upset, I mean."

I was so shocked by this I almost laughed. "You're serious, Emma? Because you always said your mom was crazy."

She blinked. "Um, I don't think you should be saying that, actually."

"I didn't say it. You did."

"Yeah, well, I'm *supposed* to complain about my mom, aren't I? And you know Becca really hurt her, Mari."

I almost said *Well, she started it*. But something in Emma's eyes told me there was no point arguing. And anyway, all I wanted too was for things to be "back to normal" between us, and it seemed like the more we talked about our moms, the more they were taking over.

And the thing is, they really were. That week word about Mom's performance had spread all over town, thanks mainly to Trisha Hartley, who was not only the vice president of the middle school PTA but also assistant head of the Youth Soccer League. I never understood how Mrs. Hartley managed to tell the story without making herself look at least a little bit responsible; after all, even if Mom had some sort of vendetta against her, you'd think there'd have to be some reason *why*. But it didn't seem as if anybody ever asked what started the whole thing. It was just like people assumed that because Mom was unicycling on the soccer fields and reciting her "LICE" poem at the Two Beez, she was nuts enough to pick on Trisha Hartley for absolutely no good reason.

So then things got ugly. We started getting crank phone calls, not just loud-breathing hang-ups in the middle of the night, but also kids shouting, "HI, CAN WE TALK TO NU-TRISHA?" Once somebody left a paper bag full of rotten tomatoes at our door. Smashed-up vegetables appeared every other day in our mailbox. Moms I didn't know frowned at me at the bus stop. And one time Sarah Wong and Ally Ferrara (who by now were back to being BFFs again) actually sat with me on the bus.

"Uh, Marigold, maybe this is none of our business, but did your mom have some sort of public meltdown?" Ally asked.

I pretended to search for something in my backpack. "You mean at the coffeehouse?"

They looked at each other. "We're not sure where it happened," Sarah admitted. "Just that it was a little . . . extreme."

I could feel my eyebrows getting sweaty. "It wasn't a public meltdown, you guys. It's just what my mom does."

I suddenly realized how wrong that sounded. Like:

My mom wasn't just crazy on that one special occasion. She's ALWAYS crazy. "She's a performance artist," I added quickly. "She was just doing one of her characters."

Ally gave me a quick smile, like *Sure she was, Marigold.* And then without saying another word, they both got up and took a seat at the back of the bus.

A couple of days after that, Matt asked if it was true that my mother was "out to get Emma's mom."

"Are you insane?" I demanded. Which I knew was a stupid way to talk to your crush, but by then I was kind of losing it.

"No," Matt answered. His gorgeous blue eyes looked worried. "But Emma's mom is saying that your mom *is.* And she's telling everyone not to let their kids come to your house. I heard that from my little brother."

"Your *brother*?" Matt's brother was in fourth grade. He'd never even met Mom. "That's just completely moronic," I argued, then pinched myself for calling his brother a moron.

And the worst thing of all was when Kennedy came home from school in tears one day because some kid in her class had told her that Mom was "dangerous and would probably go to jail."

"Mom's not going to jail," I said, giving her a hug.

"But what if they arrest her?"

"No one's going to arrest her."

"But what if Mrs. Hartley calls the cops?"

I shrugged. "The cops will say she started the whole thing."

"But what if they arrest Mom anyway? Because she made it worse."

"Then we'll go live with Dad." And I immediately changed the subject before Kennedy could point out that Dad didn't really "live" anywhere specific, and was currently "on assignment" in New Zealand.

I got us through the next hour or so by working on my patchwork Thing while Kennedy made patterns with the scraps. Finally Mom came home from a new workshop she'd just started over at the community center. As soon as she heard what that kid had said to Kennedy, she crossed her arms like a genie. "Well, that settles it," she announced. "We're moving."

"*What?*" I shouted.

"We're not sticking around this mean-spirited, gossip-mongering, nowheresville little town. We're outta here, baby."

"You're serious? Because of some dumb thing a kid said in Kennie's class?"

"Words hurt," Mom said, shaking her head. "Words are powerful, powerful weapons, Marigold."

My jaw dropped. This was being said by the person who'd taken Mrs. Hartley's own words and put them in the mouth of Nu-Trisha?

"That's exactly what *you* do," I sputtered. "Use words to hurt."

"No," she said firmly. "Sometimes I use strong words to provoke. Or to make a statement. But never merely to *hurt*. And I refuse to live in an environment where people are using negative, spiteful words about me to injure my children."

My throat was starting to burn. "You know what, Mom? Leaving my best friend behind will injure me worse."

"Mari." She reached out to touch my shoulder, but I twitched it away. "Listen, baby, I know you girls are so close. I know how important Emma is to you, and I feel terrible about all this, believe me. But wherever we move, you can stay in touch with her, can't you? There's the phone, and e-mails and IMs—"

"Emma's mom is really strict about online. She says it's a big waste of time."

"Seriously?"

"And Emma doesn't have a cell. She had one, but—"
I shook my head. "This totally isn't fair!"

"No, baby, you're right, it isn't." Her face puckered,
and she was quiet. Then she pretended to smile. "Oh,
Mari, everything will be okay. I *promise* you that. And
I'm sure you'll make great new friends wherever we go."

"What if I don't want to?"

"You never want to make new friends? Where's your
spirit of adventure?"

"I don't have one," I answered. "I *hate* all this moving. And anyhow maybe this whole thing will blow
over."

"Marigold," Mom said, suddenly looking tired. "You
know Emma's mother. Do you really think she'll ever
let this blow over?"

I thought about the hair in Emma's hairbrush. And
the look in Emma's eyes when she'd told me how her
mom was "incredibly upset."

"No," I murmured. "Probably not."

And three weeks later we were in Lawson, unpack-
ing boxes.

Soon This Will All Seem Normal

Since the minute we left Aldentown, Mom's official line has been: *I'm convinced that Trisha Hartley is an evil, dangerous person and I hope never to cross paths with her again. But Emma is fantastic, and I want you to know, Mari, that I hope you two will stay best friends forever.*

In reality, though, today is the second time Mom "forgot" to tell me that Emma had called. (The first time was the day we moved; I found out about it when Emma e-mailed me about a week later.) I wonder what's behind Mom's memory lapses: Does she think if I speak to Emma, Mrs. Hartley will snatch away the phone and say nasty things to me about My Crazy Mother?

Or: Is Mom finally feeling guilty about the Two Beez incident, and trying to pretend that the whole thing never happened?

Or: Is she "helping" me "adjust" to Life in Lawson by acting like, *Emma who? Just make a new BFF right here!*

Or: Does she just "have a lot on her mind," the way Kennie said? Of all the possible excuses, this one seems the lamest. I mean, Mom has a big brain crammed with miscellaneous stuff she's memorized, like *Hamlet* and the U.S. Constitution. She's hopeless about things like school calendars, but could she really "forget" a call she personally answered twenty minutes before I walked in the door?

I just can't believe that. And all the other excuses are almost as bad.

I am definitely not happy with her right now.

But, I tell myself, at least she opened the crate and left the kitchenette with Beezer as soon as I started dialing Emma's number. That's one decent thing about her: All her Constitution-worship makes her a fanatic about personal privacy. So she never eavesdrops. Or spies. And you'll never hear her screeching for me to get off the phone, the way Mrs. Hartley does with Emma.

I walk into the living room calling, "MOM? I'm off the phone now!"

But she's not there. I go into my bedroom. Kennie's sitting at the desk frowning at her homework.

"Mom's doing Evening Walk," she tells me. "She said she wanted to start before the snow gets too deep."

"Oh, great."

"What's wrong? You wanted to go with her?"

"Not exactly." The truth is, I was hoping that by now she'd feel guilty—if not about Emma, then about not laundering the chicken-pox shirt and the seventies track pants. So I was thinking that maybe, just to be nice, she'd decide to dogwalk past Cyndi's 24 Hour Wash'n'Go, where we use the machines.

But the ugly infirmary clothes are still on my bed where I left them, right beside my Thing. Which means Mom didn't take them with her. Which means, obviously, that I should just wash them myself. Or incur the wrath of the school nurse.

I toss them in the bathroom sink and squirt them with Ultra Concentrated Joy. Then I spread them out on the radiator and pray they'll dry by the morning.

That night when we're lying in bed, Kennedy says, "Marigold? Do you think you'll ever see Emma again?"

"Sure," I say softly.

"Do you think she'll visit? And maybe sleep over sometime?"

"I hope."

"I hope so too."

We don't say anything.

Then Kennedy says, "I don't think Mom should have made fun of Mrs. Hartley like that."

"Yeah," I say. "Well."

"I reckon she's ever so sorry."

I don't even correct her for prairie-talking.

"She is, Mari," Kennedy insists.

"If you say so." I lean over and push open the curtains just a little, so I can see the snow fall. "Isn't the snow pretty?" I say, mostly to change the subject.

"No."

"You don't like it? Why not?"

"I hate it here," Kennedy says in a tiny voice.

"You do? Why?"

"There's a mean girl in my class named Dexter. She said Kennedy is a stupid name."

"Yeah, well, *Dexter* isn't much better. Besides, Kennedy is the name of a president."

"I said that to her." She sighs. "Anyway, my school is

too big. I kept getting lost today. I couldn't even find the toilet until after gym."

"You'll figure it out. Soon this will all seem normal."

"You know what, Mari? I don't think it ever will." She rolls over on her creaky mattress. "Well, good night."

"Night."

For a long time I watch the snow coming down in big, quiet flakes. I think about making snow forts in Aldentown with Emma, Will, and Matt. It's the same snow as here, I tell myself, even though it feels different. Different in a way that will probably never feel normal. Not even if we live here for seventy-five years.

In the morning the nurse's clothes are as stiff as cardboard. And they smell like a combination of radiator rust and Joy.

"What's wrong with that material?" asks Kennedy, as I hold up the chicken-pox shirt.

"I don't know!"

She comes over to the radiator and touches the hot material. "Maybe it baked overnight."

"I'll tell you exactly what's wrong," says Mom, clomping into the living room in her snow boots. "You didn't rinse out the soap, Marigold."

"Yes I did!"

"Well, not enough, apparently. Why didn't you just wait for me to throw them in the laundry?"

"Because you wouldn't! And they had to be returned today! I told you that yesterday!"

"Calm down. Why are you so stressed out about this, anyway?" She holds up the track pants. They hang weirdly in the air, like the American flag that the astronauts planted on the moon. "Yikes. You can't return these like this. Let me drop them off at Cyndi's today and you'll bring them back tomorrow."

"No! I'm supposed to give them back this morning before homeroom. I promised the nurse." As I'm arguing, I'm thinking, *Why am I making such a big deal about this? Who even cares about these stupid pants?* But for some reason, I do. I care about these stupid pants. And I refuse to let Mom act like the stupid pants don't matter.

She puts her hands on her hips. "Well. If you really can't wait until tomorrow, I think your best bet is just to wear this stuff to school."

"*What?* You want me to *wear* them? After you made me wear *pajamas* yesterday? Are you totally trying to humiliate me?"

She groans. "Marigold. *Please* let's not start with the pajamas again."

"Okay! Fine!" I wave the chicken-pox shirt. It actually crackles.

"My point is," Mom says calmly, "if you walk to school today, the natural humidity from your body will loosen up the fabric. By the time you get to school, the material won't be so stiff. Then you can change into some regular clothes and return these to the nurse."

"That sounds like a good plan," Kennedy says hopefully.

I shrug. Actually, it kind of does.

So then I put on the nurse's clothes. They're so straight and cardboardy I can barely move.

"You look like Frankenstein," Kennedy says, giggling. "Or the Tin Woodsman. Or wait. What's the name of that robot in *Star Wars*?"

"C-3PO," I mutter. But it's good to hear her laugh, for a change.

Mom offers to walk with me, and I decide not to fight her on this because by now I'm feeling guilty about yelling at her before. She puts Beezer on his leash, we drop off Kennedy at her bus stop, and then pick up Tristan and Darla for Morning Walk.

Finally all five of us (two humans, three dogs) start the long, icy, uphill walk to school, with only one time-out for leash de-tangling. Mom walks Beezer and Darla, and I walk Tristan. Who, I quickly discover, is a definite yanker, so I have to keep his leash long enough so that he doesn't freak out, but short enough so that I'm in control. It's tricky at first, but finally we settle into a good dogwalking rhythm. And Mom is actually right: The more I walk, the more the clothes loosen up, to the point where they almost feel like clothes. I only hope they're not too sweaty by the time I get to school.

"So how's the social thing going?" Mom asks casually, just as we're getting close to the main entrance of Crampton Middle. As you've probably figured out by now, she has this flair for dramatic timing.

"It's okay," I say.

Two buses pull up right in front of the school, one right after the other. The first bus opens its doors, and out comes Brody. "Hey, Bananas," he calls, crashing on purpose into Ethan, who pushes him back. Layla follows them both, her shoulders swaying, looking like maybe she's listening to her iPod. Then the second bus opens and Quinn rushes out. I wave at her, but she runs past without saying hello, without lifting her head, even.

"You're friends with that girl?" Mom asks, darting her eyes at me.

"Not really. We just had lunch together yesterday."

"That sounds like friends."

"Maybe."

"So she *might* be a friend?"

"I don't know."

"Is she nice?"

"I guess."

Mom sighs a little puff-cloud. "Boy, I really cherish these mother-daughter chats," she says. "So much sharing. And how was Emma?"

"Emma's great." I reel in Tristan, who's sniffing an empty Gatorade bottle rolling around a dirty snowdrift.

Mom tugs on the earflaps of her rainbow-striped sherpa hat. Then she takes the leash from me and winds it three times around her mittens. "Is she still mad at me?"

"She says she isn't. We couldn't talk a whole lot."

"How come?"

"She had to hang up." Then for some moronic reason I add, "Her mom doesn't want her on the phone with me."

"What? Are you kidding me? *Why?*"

I shrug. It's not often I can shock Mom, so as long as I've opened my mouth about this, I might as well get the full effect. "We have to sneak IMs. But her mom looks over her shoulder a lot, so we can't even do that very much."

"But that's outrageous!" Mom explodes. "That woman is completely bonkers. First she bad-mouths me all over town, then she forces us to move, and now she's punishing you and Emma? Long-distance? For *what*?"

"Well," I say, kicking some ice. "You kind of do know."

She shakes her head angrily, sproinging the hair under her hat. "Look, Mari. Even if, okay, so I got a little carried away with Nu-Trisha, does this give her the right to wreak revenge on my daughter? Months after the performance? And I'm not even mentioning what she's doing to her *own* daughter." She jerks Darla's leash. "You know, I kept my mouth shut after Nu-Trisha, I thought I needed to take the high road, but enough is enough. It's time to sit down with Trisha Hartley and have a serious talk."

Suddenly my eyebrows burst into sweat. "Don't," I beg.

"Why not? Are you afraid of her?"

I shake my head.

She frowns. "Don't be such a scaredy cat, Marigold. We're not even *in* Aldentown anymore. What do we have to lose?"

"Emma," I blurt out. "I could lose Emma, okay? She *hates* big confrontations. Promise you won't call her mom or e-mail or do anything. *Please.*"

Mom makes a sound like laughing. "You don't trust me to have a civil conversation?"

"Truthfully?"

"Marigold, give me a little credit, okay? I'm a performer; I can do Rational Adult, you know."

Except you won't.

Mom stares at me, like she's reading my mind. "All right, beloved daughter," she says, her breath making a small storm cloud. "It's time for a major life lesson. Whenever someone is getting in your face, you need to look 'em right in the eye and speak out. I'm not saying you have to shout at them—"

"Mom." Jada, Ashley, and Megan are getting off the second bus. They wave at me, smiling. Ulp. I have GOT to get out of these clothes.

"But you *do* need to let them hear that they can't just trample all over you. You need to stand up and—"

"*Mom.*" I grab her sleeve. "Can we finish talking about this later? I really have to go now."

She looks shocked again. "But this is important, Mari. Wait."

"Can't," I say, and run into the building.

Inside Out

The first thing I do in the girls' bathroom is check for pointy black boots.

But there aren't any. The place is empty. Even so, I choose the wheelchair stall, which is so big it's off in its own corner, like a private dressing room. As soon as I lock the door, I pull off the track pants. They still smell like Joy, but they're a whole lot easier to take off than they were to put on. So if I hurry, I tell myself, I can return them to the nurse before homeroom. Maybe even slip them in her closet before she shows up for the day.

I stuff the pants into my backpack. I'm just about to zip up my jeans when the bathroom door bangs open.

Ashley's voice: "Did you see what she was wearing just now?"

Megan's voice: "You mean those hideous pants?"

Ashley's voice: "The whole thing, including that top. It's like something out of Gymboree."

Jada's voice: "Oh, who cares what she's wearing. She's a total zero; just ignore her."

Oh no. They're talking about ME. They have to be.

Megan: "Well, good for you, Jada."

Ashley: "Yeah. I don't know how you can be so big about this. If it was me, I'd be furious."

Jada: "What for? It won't change anything. She did what she did."

Which is what? What did I do?

Megan: "I still can't believe how nervous she was yesterday. Like we're supposed to pity her."

Jada: "I don't. I don't even want to look at her."

Ashley: "But don't you want to tell her off?"

Jada: "Why? So she can go running to her mommy?"

Hey, don't worry about that!

Ashley: "No. So she can understand how you feel."

Jada: "She totally ruined my life, okay? There's nothing to understand. And honestly, you guys? As far as I'm concerned, Quinn doesn't even exist."

When I hear the name *Quinn*, I gasp. (I mean, of course I'm relieved that they're not talking about *me*, but Quinn? Excuse me? Ruining Jada's *life*?) Then to cover up the gasp, I cough. Then I clear my throat.

The bathroom suddenly gets quiet. Maybe three seconds later, there's whispering.

"Helloooo?" Ashley calls loudly.

I freeze.

"Yoo-hoo. We know you're in there. *Hello?*"

I yank off the chicken-pox shirt and pull on my Wile E. Coyote tee. Then I sort of shuffle out of the wheelchair stall like, *Yawn, I just woke up.*

"Oh, hi," I say casually. I pretend to clear my throat again, but this just makes me sound like Mr. Hubley, so I stop.

"Marigold?" Jada is staring. "Was that you?"

"Uh-huh."

"Were you listening to us?"

"What? No," I say, my brain scrambling for an explanation. How could I possibly be hanging out in the wheelchair stall and not hear a single word of their conversation? *Improvise,* I hear Mom's voice say. *Just see where it takes you.* "I was meditating. I always meditate before homeroom."

90

Megan laughs. "Seriously?"

"Oh, yes. I do a ton of yoga. It centers me."

They stare.

"And grounds me. And helps me . . . *(focus!)* focus."

Ashley points at my chest. "Like on getting dressed?"

"What?"

"Your top is inside out."

"Oh." I look down. "Whoops." Another wardrobe fiasco, and I can't even blame this one on Mom.

"That's really, really embarrassing," Ashley points out. "You should be so glad we noticed."

"I am. Thanks a lot."

"Because two days in a row . . ." She looks at Megan, who shakes her skinny head like, *Yeah. What a loser.*

My eyebrows spring into action.

"Listen, Marigold," Jada says, fixing me with her hyper-sympathetic brown eyes. "In case you *did* overhear our conversation, and I'm not accusing you of spying or anything, you should probably know we were talking about Quinn Rieger."

"Okay," I say quickly. I pretend to be flicking my hair out of my face, but actually I'm wiping sweat droplets before they start running down my nose. "Thanks for telling me. But it's actually none of my—"

"You two had lunch together yesterday," Ashley interrupts. "Don't you remember?"

They were watching where I sat? "Oh, right. I did. She doesn't say very much."

"That's what you think," Megan says.

"Anyway." Jada smiles at me sweetly, "You just moved in and you don't really know anyone yet. So trust us on this: Be incredibly careful."

"Okay, thanks," I say. Flick.

"Don't feel sorry for Quinn," Ashley says. "And make sure you don't tell her anything superpersonal."

Megan nods. "And no matter how innocent she acts or what she says—"

The bathroom door bangs open. It's Layla. When she sees us, she grunts. Then she marches into the middle stall and slams the door.

Ashley and Megan give each other a look, but Jada just keeps smiling at me. "We can talk about this later," she says. "We'll save you a seat at lunch."

"Thanks." That's it, I have GOT to stop using this word. "But I sort of made plans today," I add desperately.

"Okay, so tomorrow," Jada says, like she's writing it on her mental calendar. "Well, you guys, it's almost home-room; we'd better go. Don't forget your top, Marigold."

Then *poof*, the three of them are gone.

I let out a long, overdue breath and catch myself in the mirror. Not only is my tee inside out, but my jeans are unzipped, and my hair is all mussed and staticky from pulling clothes over my head. I look like an electrified zombie, which leads directly to the question: Why does Jada want me to eat at her table? So she can tell me more scary things about Quinn? What if I really, really don't want to hear them?

The middle stall door bangs open.

Layla looks surprised. "You're still here."

"Uh, yeah," I say.

"Why? Don't you want to run after them?"

"What for?"

"To join the pack."

"Excuse me, but I'm not a dog."

"I didn't say you were a *dog*," Layla says, squirting soap on her hands. "I just meant Jada never travels alone." She rinses carefully, then rubs her hands dry on her ripped jeans. "So? You're going to sit with them tomorrow? And the day after? And the day after that?"

This is so insane I have to laugh. "I don't plan my lunches three days in advance. Why are you asking?"

She shrugs. She checks her mascara in the mirror. "I

think your shirt looks cool like that," she says.

"You do?"

"Yeah. Inside out is ironic."

Great. Now my cheeks are burning. "It's not supposed to be ironic. It's Wile E. Coyote."

"Oh." She runs her hands through the orange streak in her hair. "Then you actually like cartoons."

"Just classic Looney Tunes. And *The Simpsons*. Why? Is that okay with you?"

"Hey, like whatever you want." She turns and looks right into my eyes, almost the way Mom does. "Quinn didn't do anything wrong," she says seriously. "So don't believe what Jada tells you."

"She didn't tell me anything," I protest, but Layla is already gone, kicking the door open with her pointy black boots.

Greasy Fingers

I'm usually an expert at imagining disaster, but all morning long, whenever I wonder what Quinn could have done to *totally ruin Jada's life,* I draw a blank. And not because of what Layla said about not believing Jada; because somehow I know in my stomach that Quinn is innocent. I keep peeking at her—the way she tucks her wispy hair behind her ears, the way she chews on the cap of her pen, the way she looks up from her desk every once in a while, like she's afraid to catch people giving her the evil eye. But no one is ever looking at her; no one is even talking to her except Layla, and in class Layla is not what you would call chatty.

And then I watch Jada, laughing loudly, talking loudly, surrounded not just by Megan and Ashley, but by a rotating bunch of fashionista girls, and also a few of the jockiest boys. There's no way, I tell myself, that Quinn could be terrorizing Jada. Because just look at them: Alpha Girl and Outcast. Popular, Powerful, Pretty Girl and Girl Who Looks Like She's Going to Puke.

And I think: *Whoa. Now I'm sounding just like Mom.* Deciding who's right and who's wrong, who's good and who's bad, based on zero information, on how my stomach feels. I should stay out of this war, because I can't possibly have any clue what's going on. Also (no: *mainly*) because my only goal at Crampton Middle should be to keep a low profile, not make any enemies, and ride out what's left of the school year.

So at lunch I get a tray and park it smack in the middle of four girls from my gym class. They smile in a nice way and ask how it's going, how do I like Crampton so far, and isn't it gross how much the gym teacher sweats? Then they start talking about some TV show I don't watch. I'm thinking okay, well, who cares if I'm in the conversation, at least I've got camouflage, like a black-and-white horse hanging out in a herd of zebras.

But all of a sudden this fifth girl runs over and drags them off to a different table. Which means now I'm sitting here, exposed, surrounded by four deserted seats. And three tables away, Jada and Ashley and Megan and maybe ten of their closest friends are eating pizza, laughing their heads off. I'm pretty sure they haven't spotted me yet, but it's probably just a matter of time.

"These taken?" someone demands. I look up. Layla is standing in front of me, scowling, not even holding a tray. Incredibly, Quinn is right behind her, balancing a small leaning tower of Tupperware containers.

"I don't think so. They were taken a minute ago," I add, as if that matters.

They sit. Quinn tucks her wispy hair behind her ears and starts disassembling her tower. Layla rests her chin on her knuckles. She's wearing silver thumb-rings, and I see her ears have, like, six studs per lobe.

"You fixed your top," she announces.

I don't answer.

"It was better before. When you couldn't see the picture, it was kind of mysterious."

"I thought you said it was ironic."

"Ironic, mysterious. Whatever. So how's your lunch?" She narrows her smudgy eyes at my sandwich.

I shrug. "It's okay."

"That's it? That's, like, your complete review of our four-star cuisine?"

"It's turkey. There's not much to say about it."

"Yeah, there is. Sure there is. Be poetic. *It tastes like old socks. It tastes like belly button lint. It tastes like warmed-over sewage with a subtle splash of Windex*—"

"Layla," Quinn says softly. "Leave her alone, okay?"

"Hey, I'm just trying to make conversation. Why does she always have to be so snarky?"

Me? This girl is like the Supreme Goddess of Snark, and she's calling *me* snarky?

"It's just a school sandwich," I say in a jokey way. "What do you want me to say: *This sandwich reminds me of Paris, the long walks we took in the rain, that little café near the park . . . ?*"

Layla guffaws. "Yeah," she says. "That's exactly what you should say."

For some strange reason now I feel proud of myself, like it's a huge big deal I made her laugh. I nibble on my flabby bread crust and watch Quinn stir the food inside the containers, then carefully unfold a napkin. It's fascinating, like a Japanese tea ceremony, which I know about because Dad photographed one once.

Quinn notices I'm staring at her. "I'm vegan," she explains, like she's apologizing. "That means—"

"She eats veegs," Layla interrupts. She sticks her fingers into one of the containers. "Yum, yum. Zitty."

"*Ziti,*" Quinn corrects her. "With tamari sauce. Use a fork, Layla, okay?"

"I hate forks." She pops a drippy ziti into her mouth. "In fact, I've decided that from now on I'm anti-utensil."

"Really?" I say. "Why?"

"Why not? They didn't use them in the Middle Ages."

That's so illogical I have to smile. "Who's talking about the Middle Ages?"

"I am," Layla says. "The Middle Ages *rock*." She grabs one of Quinn's carrot sticks and points it at my chest. "Want to join my Jousting Club?"

"Excuse me?"

"I'm starting one this spring. It'll be much, much funner than all that regular after-school crap." She smirks. "So? Are you signing up?"

"Not if you joust with greasy fingers."

"Hey, I never said I was anti-napkin."

All of a sudden someone barks, "Yo, Bananas, move over." And takes over the empty space next to me before I can say, *Don't call me Bananas* or *There isn't any room,*

Brody. Ethan sits down too, across from Brody, who shoves his tray in the middle of the table, like he owns it.

Then he gobbles a giant bite of cheeseburger and grins so you can see smears of ketchup on his teeth.

"Okay, that's it," Layla announces. "I have just now officially become a vegan."

"Actually, I don't think they had vegans in the Middle Ages," I say.

Everyone looks at me.

"Hey, Bananas speaks," Brody says. He wipes his mouth with the back of his hand. "Awesome."

"Of course she *speaks*, you salivating carnivore," Layla says. "She's a poet."

"Yeah? Cool. Then let's hear a poem."

"Brody," Ethan says. "Shut up."

"Why? I like poems."

"No, you don't. And she's new here; give her a break."

Right then is the first time I take a good look at Ethan. He's never sat semi across from me before, so I've never noticed his dark eyelashes, or the golden freckles on his cheeks. Dark eyelashes, dark eyes, and *golden freckles*. Whew, what a combination. Plus he's standing up to Brody, which means he's smart and not a follower and amazingly *on my side*.

Okay, so now I *have* to talk to Emma.

"I don't mean sucky poems," Brody is arguing. "I mean the good kind. You know. *There once was a monkey from Spain—*"

"Much smarter than Brody's dumb brain," Layla finishes. She takes another ziti and wiggles it in front of Brody's nose. "And here it is," she says, grinning. "Your brain."

"Get that out of my face."

"No."

"Get it out, Layla."

Wiggle, wiggle. "First apologize to Marigold."

"Layla, it's fine," I say.

"No, it isn't. He's been acting like such a pig to you."

"Hey, I'm serious," Brody says, trying to grab Layla's arm.

She stands, laughing, and switches hands, still dangling the ziti. "So am I, pig. Stop the monkey jokes—"

"Layla," Quinn says.

"Or face me in a joust. I'm warning you, pig."

I'm about to protest again when boom, it hits me: *Layla and Brody are actually enjoying this. They're not fighting, they're flirting.*

Oh.

All of a sudden, Brody reaches up and bats the ziti

out of his face. It goes flying across the lunchroom and lands smack on Jada's table.

"Great," Brody mutters. He looks at Layla like, *Now are you happy?*

She blinks at him, too surprised even to laugh.

Somebody yells, "Ewwwww."

Somebody else yells, "What was THAT?"

Ashley and Megan whip their heads around. As soon as they notice Layla standing, they poke Jada and start whispering. Then Jada gets up, and with the whole seventh grade staring at her, she marches in our direction.

She's holding the ziti between her thumb and index finger, like it's a bloody severed pinky. "Did you throw this at me?" she asks Layla in a supersweet voice.

"No," Layla answers, looking Jada right in the eye.

"Yes, you did. Of course it was you. Don't lie."

Layla snorts. "You know what, Jada? If I threw it at you, I'd say so."

"No, you wouldn't," Jada says nicely, smiling through her no-braces teeth. "Because that would be admitting you did something gross and immature and trashy, and we all know how you like to pretend you're sooo cool."

Layla opens her mouth. You can hear everybody in

the whole grade suck in lunchroom air, and then let it out slowly like, *Ooooh, this is gonna be gooood.*

But what's incredibly bizarre is that Layla doesn't make a sound. I mean, literally nothing comes out of her mouth, not a single word, not even one of her snorts. She just stands there, her cheeks getting redder and redder, clashing weirdly with the bright orange streak in her hair. Finally she plonks down on the bench, scowling at Brody, who refuses to make eye contact.

Jada flips her perfect no-split-ends hair over one shoulder and glances at Ethan, who's concentrating hard on his bowl of chili. Then she leans over the table and drops the ziti into Quinn's Tupperware. "I think this is yours," she says.

"Sorry," Quinn murmurs. "It was an accident."

"Did you say something? I can't hear you."

"I said it was an accident."

"What?" Jada says distractedly, like Quinn is whispering from a distant galaxy.

Ethan puts down his spoon. "You heard her fine, Jada. She said it was an ac—"

"Oh, right, I'm *sure.*" Jada rolls her eyes. Then all of a sudden she notices I'm there. "Marigold," she exclaims.

"I told you I'd save a seat at my table. What are you doing with these total zeroes?"

"Eating a sandwich," I answer. "It's not bad, actually."

She stares at me.

"Turkey," I explain, and take a big bite.

Marshmallows

The second Jada starts walking away, Layla glares at Brody. "I hate you," she hisses.

"Why?" he says, like he's shocked. "What did *I* do?"

"Totally nothing. You just sat there. *Quinn* said something. Even *Marigold* got in her face."

"No, I didn't," I say quickly.

Layla ignores me. "You know what, Brody? Don't talk to me anymore."

Then she gets up and bangs out of the lunchroom.

After lunch she cuts science, which is a stupid thing to do, because, of course, Mr. Hubley is the homeroom teacher, so he knows she isn't absent. She shows up sixth period for math, but she spends the whole class with her head on her desk, not looking at Brody, who keeps trying to tell her obnoxious jokes, not talking to anybody, not even Quinn. All afternoon long, I can tell Ashley and Megan are buzzing around repeating everything that happened at lunch, as if the whole grade wasn't there and anybody needed an instant replay. But at least the day passes without any more drama. And as soon as the bell rings for dismissal, I grab my jacket and race out of the building.

But I don't get very far. Because the first thing I see when I step out the door is Beezer, whose leash is tied to the flagpole.

Immediately he starts barking at me like his tail is on fire. I run over, stroke his bristly fur, repeat his name a million times, but nothing works. He's barking louder now, and I'm starting to panic. How long has he been here? *Why* is he here? And where exactly is Mom?

Then I notice a yellow index card duct-taped to the flagpole:

> Hi, my name is Beezer. I'm a
> friendly beagle, with a fascinating

story about how I lost my ear.
I'll tell it to you sometime,
if you ask politely.

I'm here with Becca Bailey, mom
of Marigold (7th grade). Becca's
inside, chatting with Mr. Shamsky.
She'll be out in a few minutes,
but if I seem unhappy, please
bring me into his office.

Thanks. You're a pal.
☺ Wags.

Okay, I decide. Mom is certifiable. This clinches it.

So of course I untie him. He gives me a dopey *I love you* look and starts slobbering all over my knee. A bus pulls up to the front of the school and kids are starting to trickle out of the building now, so I rip the index card off the flagpole, flip it over, and write, *HI MOM, TOOK BEEZER, M.* I duct-tape it back to the pole, yank Beezer's leash, and we're off.

I'm about a block from school when I hear someone yelling, "Marigold! Hey, wait up."

I turn around: It's Ethan. He isn't with Brody and *he's actually running toward me*.

I sneak a pat-down of my hair, just to make sure I don't have zombie-static again, and do a casual smile, like, *Fancy meeting you here*. Then I realize the word "fancy" sounds too much like Kennedy's prairie-talk, so I stop smiling and put on an *Oh hi, it's you* sort of expression.

As soon as he catches up to me, he says, "Nice dog," and pets Beezer's head with a snowy glove.

"He isn't mine," I blurt out.

"Oh, yeah?"

"We're just . . . friends." But of course that sounds idiotic, and it doesn't explain where Beezer was all day, or how he showed up at dismissal with his leash. So I confess about Mom's note, how I have no idea what's going on. Ethan listens and nods like, *Yeah, people's moms tie one-eared dogs they don't own to school flagpoles all the time around here*. Then we watch Beezer pee on a tree trunk.

"So," he says, once we start walking again. "What do you think about Crampton?"

"It's . . . interesting," I say carefully.

"It's weird. It wasn't always weird. Just this year."

I yank on Beezer, who's sniffing someone's mailbox. "What's so special about seventh grade?"

"I don't know. Everyone's crazy all the time. Fighting over the stupidest things." I watch him pack a perfect snowball. "Like at lunch today."

He tosses the snowball into the street, a far throw that just misses a dented-up minivan.

"Um," I say. "Speaking of lunch. Can I ask you a question?"

"Sure."

"Why was Jada so mad? I mean, it wasn't even a food fight. It was just one piece of ziti. And it didn't even hit her."

"Yeah, well." He packs another snowball, which he lobs in front of Beezer. "Jada's kind of paranoid lately. She's always been, like, Boss Girl around here, and she thinks somebody turned on her."

"You mean Quinn?"

He looks at me. "Who told you that?"

"Jada, actually. Before morning homeroom." Ethan raises his eyebrows, and for some strange reason, even though I've been avoiding information all day, I decide to keep going. "So what happened?"

"Hey, this is girl stuff. I don't know all the details."

We're at a crosswalk and cars are coming, so he stops to scratch Beezer's one ear. Then suddenly he says, "All

I heard was that Jada's parents were fighting really bad. Not like, call-the-police bad, but totally screaming at each other. And Jada freaked out, so she called Quinn—"

"Why would she?"

"Why *wouldn't* she? They've known each other since preschool. We all do, basically. You know, small town."

I nod. Because I know all about small towns.

"And she made Quinn swear not to tell anyone. Jada's mom is PTA head, and Jada didn't want any gossip. But Quinn was upset, I guess, and her mom forced it out of her."

I keep nodding.

"Yeah," Ethan says. "And then Quinn's mom told Brody's mom, who, you know." He kicks some ice. "I mean, she's a nice lady and everything, but she *talks* a lot. So pretty soon . . . well, you get the picture, right?"

"Right," I say. I stop nodding, though, because I'm afraid my head will fall off.

"Anyway, Jada's furious. She feels like her whole family's been outed, and it's all Quinn's fault."

I process this. It's funny to think I kind of understand Jada, but with everything I've been through lately, I have to admit I do.

I also process the fact that it's starting to snow

110

again, big wet lazy flakes that are probably sticking to my head. I swipe them away, hoping my hair doesn't go all zombified. "But why is she mad at Layla?"

"Who knows. Layla's really warped this year. Nobody likes her except Quinn, anyway."

"And Brody."

"Hey, don't ask me to explain that."

"I'm not."

Ethan shrugs. "Anyway. That was pretty cool how you stood up to Jada at lunch."

"What? No, I didn't."

"She thinks you did."

"But all I said was—"

"You didn't follow her back to her table. She *expects* that." He's looking at me with warm brown eyes. Cocoa-warm. And he has snowflakes on his lashes, which look like teeny-tiny marshmallows. And maybe his golden freckles are like dots of cinnamon—

Uh-oh, next thing you know, I'll be slobbering like Beezer. "So you think Jada's mad at me?"

"Well, sure," Ethan says, smiling a little. "You showed her up in public. And you were sitting with her archenemies. And also . . ." Now he's blushing. At least I think he is; it could just be frostbite.

"Also what?"

He kicks more ice. "Well, there was this stupid Valentine's Day dance-thing at school a couple of weeks ago. We were taking the same bus, and she asked me if I wanted to go with her, and I basically said no way."

"Oh." Now it's me who's blushing.

"It's probably not that big a deal, but you never know."

We walk a little bit more, and I can tell he's finished with the topic of Jada. Which is a relief, because the truth is, if I hear any more, I'll start feeling sorry for her. He turned her down *on the bus*? That's almost as humiliating as your mom having a "public meltdown."

Okay, not really. I guess on the Scale of Humiliations, nothing even comes close to Nu-Trisha.

Finally he stops in front of a small white house with a wooden porch all cluttered with snow shovels and beat-up-looking sleds and boots. "So here's where I live."

"Bye," I say quickly. "Thanks for . . . the walk."

"Yeah, you too." He reaches down and gives Beezer one last pet on the head. Then he looks up at me. "See you tomorrow, Marigold," he says softly, blinking the mini-marshmallows off his eyelashes.

Swish, Swish

Beezer and I run the rest of the way home. That conversation with Ethan has my brain swirling like a snow globe, and I know that the only way to settle the snowflakes is by chatting online with Emma. As soon as humanly possible.

The second I kick off my boots at the door, Kennedy informs me that Gram's cookies arrived, and also my new bag of scraps, and that there's a note from Mom on the fridge. So I turn on my computer, go to the kitchenette, grab two giant oatmeal cookies from a shoebox Gram lined with aluminum foil, and toss the bigger one to Beezer. Then I read:

Beloved daughters,

I'm meeting Mari's principal, afterward straight to theater workshop. Don't worry, I've got Beezer. Call my cell if you need me. See you at dinner (fish).

Kisses,
Mom

P.S. Save some cookies for me!!!

"Why is Mom meeting your principal?" Kennedy is asking, her eyes popping behind her glasses. "Are you in trouble?"

"Not with him."

She makes a fish-mouth. "So then why is she——?"

"Kennie," I say. "You're asking *me*?"

I take another cookie and go off to IM Emma, but she isn't logged on, probably because she's at soccer or that Anime Club or something. So I open Gram's mailer. I don't know how she comes up with all this fabric, but this time it's a bunch of pastel-plaid flannel squares, skinny strips of fruit-colored silk, and curvy shapes of iridescent green, like mutant mermaid's fins. They're fantastically weird and random, really perfect for my Thing, but right now I'm so jumpy that if I try to sew, I'll probably just prick my fingers. So to kill time I start my homework, every ten minutes or so checking to see if Emma's online. But she never is.

At seven thirty Mom bursts in the door with an extra-large box of pizza.

"Hurry, girls, supper!" she shouts. "Big exciting news."

"Beezer's fine," I answer. "In case you were wondering. He's in his crate."

She puts the pizza box on the table and tosses her jacket and her rainbow Sherpa hat on the sofa. "Thanks, Mari, I saw your note on the flagpole. Although you could have just brought him into Bob's office."

"*Whose* office?"

"Bob's. Mr. Shamsky's. Ack, what an endless workshop. All my students were just so *tight*. I think it's the weather."

I look at Kennedy, who shrugs back. We both know that there's no point trying to force anything out of

Mom; she'll tell us her "big exciting news" at the perfect dramatic moment. So I don't even ask anything the whole time we're setting the table, and choosing our slices, and Mom is blotting her pizza grease with a napkin.

Finally she takes a huge messy bite and fans her hand in front of her mouth, miming *hot*. "Yum," she says. "Extra-cheesy. So tell me everything. Did you return those horrible clothes to the nurse, Mari? Did she say anything about the material?"

"Nope."

"Well, good. I told you walking off the soap would help."

"Uh-huh." Then I just lose it. "Mom, will you *please* tell us what's going on?"

She looks at me like, *You've been my daughter for thirteen years now, Marigold. Do you really not understand how I work?* But I think she can tell I'm not in the mood for a performance, so she takes another extra-cheesy bite, puts down her slice, and wipes her mouth.

"All right, fine," she says. "It all started this morning, Mari, when we were talking about Emma. Afterward I did some good hard thinking, and here's what I realized: The reason we didn't stand a chance in Aldentown was that Trisha Hartley was part of the community and I wasn't."

"Yes, you were," Kennedy says loyally. "You taught classes—"

"No, angel, I stood apart from people. As an Artist. I guess I thought it kept me pure." She looks at her hands, stretches her fingers, and sighs. "And what happened was, when I performed Nu-Trisha, people had no idea what I was about. I mean, they knew who I *was,* they had a basic idea of what I *did,* but they didn't know me as a *person.* But they knew Emma's mom, so when she went all over town bad-mouthing me, calling me a terrible mother and whatever other nasty lie she could think of, everyone naturally took her side."

"Actually," I say carefully, "I think the real problem—"

"Mari, I'm trying to explain my thought process."

"Okay, sorry."

She furrows her brow. "*Any*way. My point is that to do my art, I have to be free to take risks. I can't worry that I'm going to offend somebody, and I can't promise that audiences are going to love every performance. But what I *can* promise is that from now on I'll do a better job of PR."

"What's that?" Kennedy asks, wrinkling her nose.

"Public relations," Mom explains. "Mixing it up with the townfolk. Being a part of the whole"—she waves one arm toward the window—"community."

Okay, now I'm starting to freak. "Mom? Why exactly were you at my school today?"

"Exactly? To talk to your principal."

Stay calm. "I know. You wrote that in Beezer's note. What about?"

"Well, I was coming to that." She takes another bite of pizza. Then she says, "In the interest of community outreach, and also to introduce our family to the neighborhood, I decided to give a free performance at your school. I was proposing Friday night in the gym."

"MOM. NO."

"Unfortunately that's what Bob said. Apparently they need the space for some kind of depressing basketball tournament or something."

"I hate basketball," Kennedy says. "We're doing it in gym and I haven't made one single basket yet. Dexter called me a spaz."

Mom frowns. "Who's Dexter?"

"A horrid girl in my class."

"Well, ignore her, then. And just repeat to yourself: *Swish. Swish.*"

"Why?"

"It's the sound of the net when the ball sails through. Just keep hearing that sound—*swish! swish!*—and you'll make the basket."

"*Swish. Swish.*"

"Say it like you mean it, Kennie. *SWISH, SWISH.* Can you hear the air vibrating?"

"Mom?" I say loudly. "So that's your big news? You asked if you could perform on Friday night and Mr. Shamsky said no?"

"Of course not," she answers, smiling. "What's so exciting about that? My news is that I'm doing a club."

"A what?"

"An after-school Improv Club, starting right after spring break. It was Bob who suggested it, actually. Apparently they offer all kinds of fun things—cooking, chess, pottery—"

Jousting with greasy fingers. "Yeah, I heard about the clubs. So what does this mean? You're planning to teach—"

"Oh, no, baby, you can't *teach* what I do. I'll just be encouraging kids to stand up in front of an audience and have fun." She pushes away her plate. "Oh, Marigold, kids your age can be so painfully self-conscious. I want to loosen them up, get them to really enjoy performing. Because you know, precious daughters, when it all comes down to it, life is really just one big improv act."

That sounds like a line she's practiced. Which is kind of ironic, actually.

"But why at *my* school?" I say, tearing off a tiny bit of crust. "I mean, can't you just keep doing your workshop at the college?"

"Sure. I plan to. But it's only three hours a week."

"Well, then, do the club at Kennie's school."

"Oh, could you?" Kennedy pleads. "That would be ever so splendid!"

Mom smiles. "The sad truth, Kennie, is that kids your age don't get what I do. Mari, you remember all that fuss in second grade, don't you?"

I shrug, even though obviously I remember perfectly. "Listen, nobody at my school will get it either. Plus they all hate each other, they're paranoid, and they overreact about *everything*."

"Oh, come on. I'm sure it's not so bad."

"That's because you don't go there. It's like a giant war zone."

She laughs, but it's not a ha-ha laugh. "Okay, now you're being slightly overdramatic."

I stare at her. "*I'm* overdramatic?"

She folds her arms across her chest and pushes her chair back from the table. "All right, Marigold. Is there something you want to say here?"

"Marigold," Kennie says softly. "I truly think you should hush."

I look at Mom. Her eyes are glowing, like she's in the middle of a big dramatic scene, and she's waiting for me to say my line.

So fine, I say it. "I don't want you teaching at my school."

"Why not?"

"Because your stuff embarrasses me."

She does a gasping laugh. "It does? What stuff are you referring to, exactly?"

"Basically all of it. The whole performance thing."

"*The whole performance thing.* You're referring to what? Everything I do onstage?"

"Just about."

"Whew. Wow. You never told me you felt this way."

"You never asked."

She sits there, blinking, for once speechless and obviously shocked. Obviously hurt, too, and I'm thinking, *Why did I say all that? Should I take it back? Act like it was a dumb joke? Apologize?*

But then she looks me right in the retinas and announces, "For your information, Marigold, I happen to know the difference between performing and teaching. And if I *do* teach improv at your school, I'm sure your classmates would absolutely love it."

"That isn't the point," I say, my voice coming out squawky. "I'm asking you *not* to do it. For *me*."

"Oh, but it *is* for you! For our whole family! That's what I was trying to explain before. And it's not up to the two of us, anyway. I still have to write a proposal, and the PTA head has to approve it." Suddenly she does this big fake cheery smile. "Oh, Mari, it'll be fabulous, you'll see. Come on, have a little faith in me, all right?"

She messes my hair and kisses Kennedy on the forehead. Then she springs up from the table and does a yoga stretch so complicated I'm sure she made it up herself. "And now, beloved daughters, I need to round up my Evening Walkers. Are there any cookies left? I think I'll take some for the road."

Settle Down

The second Mom and Beezer are out the door, I run to my computer to IM Emma. But she's still logged off, even though it's 8:25, prime homework time, when we usually chat. What's going on? Where is she?

The phone rings. I snatch the receiver from the kitchenette wall.

"Emma?" I shout. "Is that you?"

"It's Dad," he says. "Sorry to disappoint you, Monster." He pauses. "Is Mom around?"

"No, she's out dogwalking."

"I was hoping you'd say that," he admits. "I kind of wanted to talk to you in private."

"You did? How come?"

"I, uh, have big news."

Okay. I don't know about you, but there's only so much big news I can handle in one day. I take the phone and sink onto the sofa. "Can I ask you a favor? Please just say it fast."

"I'm getting married."

Not that fast. "You are? To The—I mean, to Mona?"

"Who else?"

Don't ask me. You're the one with Surprise Girlfriends. "That's so great, Dad. I'm really happy for you."

"Thanks, Mari."

"When will it be?"

"This summer." He pauses. "We were hoping after the honeymoon you and Kennie could take a little trip with us. Mona knows a dude ranch out west where the three of you could relax, get better acquainted. And it's even got a vegetarian meal option."

"Sounds perfect," I lie. "Kennie loves horses; I'm sure she'll be psyched. Of course, she'll start talking like a cowboy and wearing fringes on everything."

He chuckles. "Yeah. Well, we can put up with that, right? As long as she doesn't chew any tobacco." He pauses again, longer this time. "But first I'll need to clear all this with Mom."

"Ri-ight," I say. "And does she know about you and—"

"No. Not yet. Any suggestions on how to break the news?"

"You're asking *me*?"

"Just joking," he says, but neither of us is laughing. "Well, anyway, I wanted you to be the first to know."

"Thanks, Dad."

He exhales. "Okay, love you, Monster. Can you hand the phone over to Kennie now?"

So I do, then head straight to my computer. *Log on*, I pray to Emma. *Please log on. I desperately need to talk to you.*

But she isn't there. Still. Maybe her computer is broken or something.

All of a sudden I have a crazy idea. I'll call her house. If she picks up, we'll have an actual conversation, even if it's only for a few minutes. If either of her parents answer, I'll just hang up. And I'll use my cell, so they won't be able to caller ID my house.

I step out of my bedroom and hear Kennedy's voice on the phone with Dad. She sounds like she's arguing: "*Yeah, a dude ranch sounds okay. I know you do, Daddy. But whyyyy do you have to—"* I shut the door and dial Emma's number. It rings four times. On the fifth ring, someone answers.

"Yeah-lo," says a Hartley. Not Emma, though. Definitely not Trisha, and probably not her dad. One of her slobby brothers. Can't tell who yet.

"Um," I say.

"Can you repeat that?" Okay, got it. It's Seth, the one who microwaved SpaghettiOs. I've always hated how he teases Emma, but he's usually pretty decent to me.

I clear my throat, hoping that makes my voice thick and goopy, like Mr. Hubley's. "Sorry, bad cold. Is Emma there?"

Silence. *"Marigold?"*

Dang. "Uh, yes, actually. How are you, Seth?"

"You shouldn't be calling this house."

"I know. But this'll be really quick, I swear."

He thinks; I can hear him breathing.

"Seth," I beg. "Can I *please* talk to Emma? I wouldn't call if it wasn't incredibly important."

"Whatever," he finally mutters, then hollers, *"EMMMM-AAAA!"*

For a few seconds I don't hear anything, then some

muffled voices, then the phone dropping, then Emma: *"Marigold?"* Her voice sounds almost squeaky.

"Are you okay?" I ask.

"No. Are you?"

"Me? No. That's why I'm calling. I just had a huge fight with Mom at supper. She's threatening to teach an acting class at my school. Can you believe that? I think this cute boy may like me, but also this nasty girl really hates me. And then five minutes ago Dad called—"

"Your dad?" She sounds confused now. "What *about* him?"

"That's what I'm telling you. He's marrying The Horrible Mona Woman. And dragging us off to some vegetarian dude ranch!"

She doesn't say anything.

"Emma? You there?"

"Mari," she says slowly, "I think you may not know what happened."

"What are you talking about?"

"This morning. Your mom called my mom. And basically threw a fit about my mom not letting us talk on the phone. And forcing us to sneak IMs—"

"What?"

"Becca told her we've been chatting online, so now

I can't use my computer for anything but homework. And if Mom catches me on the phone with you—" Emma starts sniffling. "This is so messed up. And it just keeps getting worse."

For a second I'm speechless. Then I sputter, "I can't believe my mom called your house. She's totally out of control!"

"So you didn't know?"

"Well, she told me she wanted to, but I begged her not to. And I thought—"

"Did she promise you she wouldn't?"

I think about our conversation this morning, how I ran off to change my pants before we'd finished. What was my big hurry? To go eavesdrop on Jada Sperry? "No, I guess not. I guess she never promised anything."

"Listen, Mari," Emma says. "Things are really bad over here. My mom's incredibly upset. Not just at your mom, but at me for sneaking online. And I hate feeling she doesn't trust me anymore."

"So what are you saying?"

"It's so unfair. But maybe we should . . . I don't know. Let things go for a while."

"Let things go? What does that mean? You're saying not be—"

"Don't get mad," she says quickly. "Okay?"

"But that's crazy, Emma! It's *wrong*. Can't you stand up to her about this?"

"Stand up about what? I *was* sneaking, wasn't I?"

"Yes, but only because she made you!"

"Okay, now you're sounding exactly like Becca."

My throat is closing up now. "Emma, how can you say that?"

"Sorry. I just mean you're acting like my mom's this big powerful villain. Even though *Becca* was the one who called. And attacked *her*."

"Mom didn't mean to attack," I say limply.

"You're *defending* her?"

"No! But she wants us to stay friends. I'm sure she just meant to stick up for us."

"Well, that's a funny way to do it." Emma blows her nose. "Anyway, I really do think we should take a break right now. Until things settle down a little. Mari?"

"Uh-huh?"

"I know this isn't your fault."

"Well, sure! Of course it's not my—"

"What I mean is, I know you didn't purposely tell Becca about the IMs. It just slipped out, right?"

I try to think of that freezing walk, what I said,

what Mom said, but right now all I remember clearly is wanting to shock her. Wanting to tell her something she didn't know.

"Yeah," I mumble. "Sort of."

Emma sighs. "Look, I'm sure you'll like Lawson if you give it a chance. You're a really great person. I'm sure if you just—"

"Don't worry, I've already made a ton of new friends. There's this boy—"

"But you said some girl hates you?"

"It's not important, Emma. I'll be fine."

Then we don't say anything. This may be our last conversation—our last anything—for a long time, so it's weird how we're both being quiet. But somehow my mouth has just stopped working.

"Okay," Emma finally says in a small voice. "Well, I'd better get off the phone now. See you, Marigold."

"You too," I whisper, and hang up just as Mom bursts in the door.

Definitely Bad

"Oh, sweetheart, what's *wrong?*" Mom asks, throwing her arms around me. She smells like dogs and snow and oatmeal cookies. For a second I let her squeeze me, resting my head against her down jacket.

Then I pull away. "Mom," I say. "Were you going to tell me you called Trisha Hartley?"

"Oh! Of course I was. But we got sidetracked at dinner about the club thing."

"And you told her about the IMs? How could you? Now she's furious at Emma."

"Oh, no. Is she really?"

"And Emma doesn't want to be friends."

"With you? She said that?" Mom looks shocked.

I nod.

"But you didn't do anything! Is Emma *blaming* you?"

"It's complicated," I answer, shrugging. "There's all this stuff between Emma and her mom."

Mom rubs my cheek with her freezing hand. "Oh, baby. This is really such a shame. And so unfair to *you*."

"Yeah, it is," I say. "Unfair to me."

And then before I figure out that it's happening, I'm crying. Mom hugs me again, and I let her this time, even though she's kind of missing the point about her role in all this.

Now Kennedy is standing in the doorway, without her glasses. Her eyes look enormous and pink.

"Kennie, can you give us a minute, please?" Mom says, handing me a linty tissue from her jacket pocket.

Kennedy nods. But she doesn't go away. "Mari told you?" she asks in a small, shaky voice.

"Yes, angel. She just now told me all about Emma."

"No, I mean about Dad."

"Kennie," I say in a warning voice. "I really don't think—"

"Think what?" Mom asks quickly.

Suddenly Kennedy bursts into tears and flings her

self onto my bed. I try to catch her eye to give her a look that means *not now,* but she's so busy sniffling and gasping that she isn't registering.

Mom looks at me, alarmed. "Okay. What *about* Dad?"

"Nothing." I wipe my eyes with my sleeve.

"Mari. *What?*"

"He's marrying Mona," Kennedy blurts out. A string of snot is dangling from her nose, so I hand her my wet tissue.

Mom turns to me, white-faced. "So," she murmurs. "And were you going to tell *me?*"

"I just found out," I say. "Dad called, like, the minute you left—"

"And you called Emma." She shakes her head. "I had my cell phone. You should have called *me,* baby."

"I know. Except I was really mad at you." I sniff in some drippy snot. "But I'm sorry I said all that stuff. About your performances."

"That's okay. I knew you didn't mean it." Mom sighs. "Well," she says tiredly. "I'd say we were all due for a Chocolate Night, but it's too cold to go out shopping again. And I ate too many of Gram's cookies, anyway."

"Me too," says Kennie, hiccupping. "Besides, now my stomach hurts."

"It does? Do you think maybe you're going to—"

"Throw up? I don't think so." But she has that look she gets, so Mom puts her arm around Kennedy's shoulders and walks her to the bathroom.

A few minutes later I hear Mom close the door to her own bedroom and make some phone calls. I can't hear very much, but it sounds as if first she's talking to Gram ("Oh, Mom, I'm just in shock"), and then to Dad ("And this is how I find out, Jeff? From the *girls?*"). After a while I check on Kennedy and she tells me she's fine, she's getting bored in the bathroom, and can she please come out? So I say sure, why not, and we put on our pj's and both pretend to fall asleep.

Next morning, Mom is in the living room, upside down, surrounded by marbles.

"What a night, huh?" she greets me. "Did you get any sleep?"

"Not really."

"Me neither. So finally around three a.m. I started writing up my club proposal. I think it's okay, but I'm not used to dealing with PTA types. Maybe after school today I can show you what I wrote?"

"I guess."

"Great! Thanks a lot, Mari. Oh, and I baked some carrot muffins for breakfast. They're pretty good, although I think I prefer more cinnamon."

Kennedy and I eat the carrot muffins in the kitchenette while Mom chatters in the living room about Cinnamon Versus Ginger, and how even though ginger is wonderful for your digestion, there's no better smell on a cold winter morning than cinnamon baking in the oven. This is a spontaneous performance, obviously; the weird thing is that I can imagine her saying the very same words as Nu-Trisha, although of course I'm not going to give her any ideas.

Finally she flips over and sends a whole bunch of marbles rolling.

"Well, precious daughters," she says, her face flushed. "Last night sure wasn't any fun, was it? But today will be better, promise. I have a big surprise for you both."

"A surprise?" Kennedy says hopefully. "You mean like Chocolate Night?"

"Oh, no. Last night was Chocolate Night, even

without chocolate. Today is a whole new day."

Meaning what? Mom's not starting a Humiliate Marigold Club? Dad's not marrying The Horrible? I'm still best friends with Emma?

Just thinking the word "Emma" makes my throat start to ache.

I push my plate away.

"Marigold?" Mom says, looking at me with question-mark eyes. "Don't you want to guess the surprise?"

"Well, if I did, it wouldn't be a surprise," I say.

She opens her mouth like she's going to answer something. But then she just shakes out her hair and pretends to smile.

"You know what, Mari? You're absolutely right" is all she says.

When I walk in the door to morning homeroom, Mr. Hubley is spitting a blob of phlegm into his hankie. It's so disgusting I'm almost wishing I'd totally skipped the carrot muffins.

"Attention, please. Settle yourselves down, people," he says. People settle themselves down, meaning they take their seats and keep talking. So he raps on the side of his desk with a rolled-up tube of papers.

"ATTENTION. We have PTA business to conduct. Jada, since this is your mom's, uh, field, why don't you pass around these, whatever they are. Forms."

Jada rolls her eyes, but she immediately gets up and hands out the forms titled SPRING AFTER-SCHOOL CLUB APPLICATION *(Want to start your own club? Please do! We encourage all Crampton Middle parents, students and teachers to design fun, worthwhile programs for our after-school program, but first you'll need PTA approval. Simply fill out the attached questionnaire. . . .)*

When Jada gets to my desk, she stops. And waits.

"Um, can I please have one?" I ask.

"What?" She looks at me with Bambi eyes.

"A form. Can I please have a form."

"Oh, *sure*," she says, smiling sweetly. Then she drops a form on my desk.

I stuff it into my backpack. Some people crumple theirs into balls and start pelting each other. Layla, I see, is hunched over hers, writing something with a stubby pencil. She's still mad at Brody, I'm pretty sure, because when he leans over to see what she's writing, she growls and hides the form under her desk.

All morning long I'm spacing out, my brain too crammed with last night to take in anything else. And then at lunch I don't even think about where to sit; I just head over to Quinn and Layla.

"You okay?" Layla asks, squinting at me through her mascara.

"Fabutastic," I say.

"I'll take that as ironic." She pushes her club application toward me. "So you're a poet. Check my spelling on this, all right?"

Name of Proposed Club or Activity:
JOUSTING CLUB

Desired Number of Students:
Infinite, but two at a time

Desired Location:
Medieval England, but will settle
for Crampton football field

Equipment Needed:
2 horses
2 tents
2 complete sets of armor
for knights

(chain mail, helmets, shield,
breastplates, arm & shoulder pieces)
2 iron shields to protect
horses' heads
2 solid oak lances
(good ones, not crappy ones)
long-necked spurs

I stop reading. "Uh, Layla? You don't really expect them to approve this, do you?"

"Of course not. My club ideas never get approved."

"So then why are you even—"

"Because," she says, grinning, "if I don't submit something, Jada's mom will be sooo disappointed."

Quinn smiles at me. Her teeth look like baby teeth. "In fifth grade Layla proposed a Yodeling Club. And last year she came up with—what was it called?"

"The Wonderful World of Condiments," Layla says in a cozy Martha Stewart sort of voice. She clasps her hands. "Every week we'd explore a different condiment: mayo, salsa, relish, guacamole."

"What about peanut butter?" I ask.

"That's a food, not a condiment," Layla corrects me. "Besides, I'm deadly allergic to peanut butter. One bite and I'm a goner." She sticks her fingers in Quinn's Tupperware, and pulls out what looks like a chunk of tofu in soy sauce. "Anyway, Jada's mom wrote me this incredibly polite note that said while she 'appreciated my enthusiasm,' she didn't think Condiments was 'an appropriate theme for a PTA-sponsored club.' So I was stuck taking stupid Origami until I got kicked out for making paper airplanes."

I have to smile. "Well, if you thought Origami was stupid, why did you bother signing up?"

"Because you have to." She wiggles her saucy fingers at me. "Or else."

Quinn hands Layla a napkin, and also a pair of those wooden chopsticks they give you in Chinese restaurants. "Mr. Shamsky made spring term into this big after-school thing," she explains. "And now the rule is, everybody has to do a club."

Oh, great, I think. Because if everybody has to do a club, someone will end up doing Mom's.

Unless Jada's mom doesn't approve. In fact, knowing how Mom writes her grant applications, with the hyper fonts and the photos and the detail-by-detail descriptions of her past performances, I can definitely see the PTA banning her from the building.

So maybe there's no reason to freak, I tell myself.

And then I think: *Yeah, but for Jada's mom to reject Mom's proposal, first she has to sit down and read it.*

Scraps

I walk into our apartment with a deal already worked out in my head (*Listen, Mom, if you forget about that improv club, I'll do anything you want. For the entire rest of my life*). But before I even take off my backpack, Kennedy comes rushing in from the living room. "Remember Mom's surprise?" she shouts. "Well, guess what, Mari! Gram's here!"

"Gram?"

"She's visiting for the weekend. Isn't that *splendid*?"

I toss my backpack, kick off my boots, and run into the living room. And here's Gram walking toward me with her arms outstretched, ready to give me a big hug.

"Marigold," she says, and I melt. Some people are

just like that, I guess. They have the magical power to warm you up. With Gram it's mainly her voice that's so warming, but it's also something special in her eyes. The funny thing is that she has the same dark eyes we all do—by "we all" I mean Mom, Kennedy, and me— but hers just have a special glow. And when she looks at you, you just relax, I guess, because you know she always likes whatever she's seeing.

She kisses my forehead and rubs off the magenta lipstick. Then she stands back and beams at me. "You've gotten taller," she says. "Also curvier."

"*Gram.*"

"Well, you have. You look gorgeous. So what have you been up to? Making new friends?"

I nod.

"Working on your quilt?"

I make a pretend-annoyed face. "It's not a quilt, Gram. I keep telling you: It's a Thing."

"Oops, I forgot," she says, smiling. "So can I take a peek at this famous Thing?"

"You mean right now?"

"Sure. You have something better to do?"

"I don't know. You just got here. Don't you want some tea or something?"

She hoots at that. "All your mom has is that god-awful ginger stuff. Besides, I didn't come all this way to drink tea."

So I lead her into my bedroom, which I suddenly wish was a whole lot cleaner. And cozier, too. I watch her take in the unmade beds, the two scuffed white desks pushed up against the foggy window, my small flower-shaped corkboard crowded with, like, twenty overlapping photos: of Dad, of Gram, of Emma. She doesn't say, *Oh, Marigold, this room could be so much nicer if . . .* But I can tell what she's thinking: *If only you'd paint it some cheery color. If only you'd tidy it up a little. If only it looked as if you and Kennedy were really settled in.*

I un-smush the Thing from the foot of my bed and carefully spread it out. It's such a funny shape that it trails onto the floor, then reaches across my pillow like a backward tentacle. And the scraps are so clashing—pink gingham, big purple flowers, kind of a sixties Pop Art print, swirly rainbow stripes, all in different shapes and sizes—that the whole thing looks sort of alarming, like some sort of mutant shape-shifting alien that's oozed all over my bed.

Still, I like it. I don't know why, but for some bizarre

reason I think it's beautiful. Beautiful and random. Beautiful *because* random.

Gram studies it for a long time, as if she's reading a hard poem. She touches it gently, running her wrinkled fingers over the fabric, smoothing out the puckers. Finally she looks at me with bright eyes.

"It's wonderful," she says. "Did you get the other scraps I sent?"

"Yesterday," I answer. "The iridescent ones are great. And the flannel ones are so soft. I'm sorry I forgot to thank you—"

She holds up a hand. "Never mind about that. But here's a question for you, cookie: Do you ever wonder where I get all this fabric?"

"Actually, yes."

"Well, then, what if I tell you. Okay if we sit a minute?"

I push aside the Thing so we can both fit on my bed, but Gram pulls the tentacle part into her lap. She strokes it a couple of times, then says, "So how are things between you and Mom these days?"

I blink at her. Gram's old, I guess, but it's not like she loses her place in conversations. So why are we suddenly talking about *Mom*?

"Sort of terrible," I admit.

She purses her lips. "What's going on?"

I tell her about Mom's phone call to Trisha, how Trisha threw a fit and now Emma doesn't want to be friends. And while I'm on the endless topic of Mom Ruining My Life, I mention the whole after-school club business. I even tell her about Pajama Day.

Gram listens to it all without saying anything. Finally she takes my hands into her lap. "I know you're going through a rough time right now," she says gently. "And I know you're used to thinking about your mom in a certain way. But you know what, honey? When I think of Becca, I see her at just about your age. She was such a creative, spirited, talented girl, and I was always very, very proud of her."

"I know that, Gram."

"But she wasn't easy. Your Uncle Robby was a piece of cake, but your mom . . ."

We both laugh a little, but the truth is, this conversation has me totally lost.

"And she was always performing," Gram says. "Locking herself in the bathroom, trying on all my makeup, and singing. Or turning her bed into a stage and making up speeches. Half the time I didn't understand what she was even doing. And if I asked her, *'Becca, sweetie, why don't you just try out for the school play,'* she'd just look at me with those big dark eyes of hers and say something like, *'Oh Ma, the school play is so boooring. Besides, I'd rather write my own lines.'* And she was so intense about everything, so after a while I just let her be."

Gram strokes my hands thoughtfully, not looking at me. "But she was always so restless," she adds. "It was as if she didn't know what she wanted."

"Not anymore," I insist. "Mom always knows *exactly* what she wants. That's the problem. She doesn't care about anything else. Or any*one*."

"You think so?" Gram says. "Let me share a little incident with you, Mari. One day when your mom was about thirteen, she closed the door to her bedroom and didn't come out." She sighs. "I didn't realize it at the time because I was busy helping your uncle with his homework. But when suppertime came, and I knocked on Becca's door, there she was, with a big pair of scissors, cutting all her favorite clothes into scraps. Just tatters, all over the floor, her bed . . ." Gram shakes her head.

"Why did she do that?" I ask, horrified. "Was she mad at you?"

"Oh, no. It had nothing to do with me. She said she

wanted to make a new kind of costume. *Something different and amazing*: Those were her exact words."

"But that's just . . . *wrong*," I sputter. "Destroying her favorite clothes—"

"She *meant* to make something special," Gram interrupts. "She wanted to take all these scraps and sew them together."

"But she can't even sew!"

"No, she can't, honey. She tried, but she couldn't get anywhere, and she just kept getting frustrated, and she refused to let me teach her. Or help her. She wanted it to be '*all her own*,' she said." Gram smiles. "You know how stubborn your mother can be. Pigheaded."

I nod.

"And then, boom: She realized what she'd done. I'll never forget how she came to me in tears, like her heart was breaking: '*Oh, Ma, I ruined all my best clothes, I'm so sorry, what a stupid idea that was, you must think I'm the worst daughter in the world.*' I tried to tell her I'd never think such a thing, but she wouldn't listen, and then she insisted on paying for her new clothes. I think she walked the neighbors' dog every day for a whole year. And eventually she just forgot about her costume idea. But I never did."

I don't say anything.

Finally I let out a long, reluctant breath. "So these are her scraps?"

Gram nods.

"And you saved them all this time? Why?"

She puts her arm around my shoulders. "I knew Becca meant them to be different and amazing. And now they are."

"But they aren't," I protest. "I just stitched them together. They don't mean anything, Gram."

She kisses my forehead and doesn't even wipe off the lipstick this time.

"They're just this dumb thing I do," I say. "To pass the time."

"Different and amazing," she repeats, like an echo.

Cross My Heart

The whole rest of the afternoon, I keep thinking about the Thing. How it's *mine,* despite what Gram said, how it has nothing to do with Mom. How all right, so it's made out of her seventh-grade clothes, but she hasn't worn this fabric in, like, thirty years, she obviously doesn't recognize any of it, and she's totally forgotten about the crazy costume idea, anyway. And why does everybody in this family always have to turn everything into big, fat, meaningful symbols? My Thing is just a *thing.* It's not a costume. It's not even a shape.

I take a good long look at the Thing, still spread all over my bed. Then I smush it into a puffy blob and tuck it beside my pillow.

After dinner I'm watching *Access Hollywood* in the living room when I realize I can hear Mom and Gram arguing. They're not shouting or anything, but they're washing the dishes, so they have to raise their voices over the running water. With the TV on also, I can make out only a few words. So I get off the sofa and tiptoe just outside the kitchenette.

"But are you sure it's healthy?" Gram is asking. "Kennedy is so skinny."

"She's skinny because she has Jeff's skinny genes," Mom answers. "Not because she's vegetarian. And anyway, she's doing fine. When she had her physical last month, the doctor said."

"But she's way too young to be choosing what she eats, Bec."

"She doesn't choose. *I* do. But I'm trying to respect her feelings."

"I know you are, but—"

"Didn't you try to respect mine when I was growing

up? Isn't that why I turned out so spectacular?" Now Mom is teasing, but I can hear the sharp edge in her laugh.

"Yes, of course," Gram answers huffily. "But there are limits. Children need protein."

"And she gets *tons* of it. Really, Ma, you can be so rigid about food."

For a second I'm afraid another big Trisha-fight is starting, but now Mom and Gram are quiet. I can hear the dishes clatter, though, like they're doing the arguing.

Then Mom says, "Sorry I called you that. I'm just kind of upset right now, and I don't want to be arguing about hamburger."

"Neither do I," Gram says. There's a pause. "Is it about Jeff?"

"Yeah." The faucet shuts off. "Although actually it's more about Marigold. I feel like she doesn't trust me anymore."

"Of course she does!"

"No, Ma, she's always mad at me. She says I embarrass her. And she barely even talks to me these days."

"She's just at that tricky age."

"Yeah, well, I talked to *you* when I was thirteen."

"Sometimes." Gram laughs. "Don't you remember giving me the silent treatment that time I showed up at your school in plaid pants?"

"No. I did?"

"You refused to talk to me for two days. And when you finally started up again, you called me *mortifying*. And that was just for starters."

Gram? Mortifying? What a horrible thing to say. And not just horrible: unfair. Because she totally understood about the costume business. Plus she saved all of those scraps, even after Mom forgot about them. So how could Mom have possibly ever thought—

"Mari? Why are you standing there?"

I spin around.

And see Kennedy walking toward me.

And realize there's something hard under my right foot.

A marble.

Before I know what's happening, I'm sprawled on the floor.

"Do you think you can walk?" Mom is asking. Her face is pale and her eyes look huge.

"Probably," I say.

I guess I'm not too convincing, though, because she and Gram insist on lifting me up and helping me hop over to the sofa. Then Gram hurries to the freezer to get some ice, while Mom carefully pulls off my sock and props up my foot with a pillow.

"It's all my fault," she's muttering. "Those stupid marbles. I had them in the box yesterday, but Beezer knocked it over. And I thought I found them all, but I guess one got away. Oh, Marigold, I'm so sorry—"

"It's okay," I say quickly. Because of course now I'm feeling scuzzy about eavesdropping on her. And I can tell Kennedy realizes that's exactly what I was doing, because she's making a fish-mouth and avoiding eye contact.

The phone rings. Beezer starts barking like crazy from his crate.

"Somebody answer that phone," Gram hollers. "I'm dealing with this god-awful ice cube tray."

Kennedy runs into the kitchenette. "Uh-huh," I can hear her say. "Uh-huh. Okay. I'll tell her." Then she hangs up and comes running back into the living room, followed by Beezer and Gram.

"Remind me to teach you some phone manners, Kennie," Mom says. "Who was that?"

"The PTA lady from Mari's school. She said your club was approved, but she wants you to call her back."

"What club?" Gram asks, catching my eye. She's holding about a glacier of ice wrapped in a towel, and now she's pressing it hard on my throbbing ankle.

"Just improv," Mom says distractedly. "Theater games, mostly."

"Her name is Lisa Sperry," Kennedy announces. "And her number is 645-7125. I wrote it on my hand." She waves her inky palm at Mom. "When are you going to call her?"

"Later," Mom says. "Or tomorrow. Sometime."

"She said it was ever so important."

"I'm sure she didn't say *ever so*," I comment. I pet Beezer, who is now slobbering on my knee. Then I turn to Mom. "And I thought you wanted me to help you with the application."

"Well, you didn't seem too eager, frankly, so I just e-mailed it in this morning." Mom stares deep into my eyes, like she's searching for buried treasure. "Listen, Mari. I've been thinking. If you really don't want me to do this club, I won't."

Kennedy looks at me. Gram doesn't.

I wince a little, so Gram takes off the ice pack. Then

I peek at my ankle: It looks perfectly normal, not swollen, not even black-and-blue.

Suddenly, in addition to feeling scuzzy, I'm feeling incredibly idiotic. Also selfish. Also drama-queeny, which is something I do *not* want to feel.

"It's *just* theater games?" I ask Mom. "You *promise* you won't do a performance?"

She shakes her sproingy hair. "No performance, Mari. Promise."

"And you won't try to sell tickets to a performance? Or use the club for free publicity? Or do anything—I'm serious, Mom, *anything*—besides teaching improv?"

Mom takes my hands in hers. "I swear, baby," she says solemnly. "I'll just teach improv. Cross my heart."

I look at Gram. Her eyes are bright, and her lips are shut tight, like she's forcing herself not to speak.

"Well, okay," I say finally. "I guess you can do the club."

Gram beams at me. So does Kennedy. Mom kisses my cheek.

"Just don't make it humiliating," I add, wiggling my toes.

Rotating Gyroscope

On Sunday after lunch I'm on my bed pretending to read *The Lord of the Rings* for English. For some dumb reason I chose it as my independent reading, but it's so boring my mind keeps wandering off in a million directions. Plus it doesn't help that Mom is on her bedroom phone, and her door is open, so I can hear every word. She's talking to Jada's mom in a fakely rah-rah sort of voice, like she's doing a new performance: Becca Bailey, PTA Volunteer.

"Oh, I'm so excited," she says. "No, I've never worked with middle school kids before. But my daughters— Two. Kennedy is eight, and Marigold is— Oh, is she? In the same homeroom? Isn't that funny. . . . No, I don't think she ever has, but you know girls this age— Uh-huh. Uh-huh. No, that makes perfect sense. I'll get on that as soon as I— Well, I'll try. But I'm not very— No, I understand. No problem. Uh-huh. Thanks for calling."

Silence.

Then Mom shouts, "AAAACK. Well, *that* woman is a major-league pain in the butt!"

"What woman?" Gram calls from the bathroom.

"Lisa Sperry, PTA czar of Marigold's school. She's demanding an itemized budget for my Improv club, ASAP." Mom groans. "And how can I possibly make a budget before I meet my kids? Because who knows, after the first session, I might decide okay, what we really need is a room-size trampoline—"

A room-size trampoline?

"And the worst part," Mom adds, "is that I'm sure she's terrorizing me just to prove she can."

"Oh, Becca," Gram is saying. "Just guesstimate about the budget. This is public school; you're not getting a trampoline even if you want one. And if this PTA lady is a little pushy, who cares. The important thing—"

I hear her walk into Mom's room and shut the

door. She's in there for a long time, like maybe twenty minutes.

The whole time they're talking. Not fighting, talking. Back and forth, but quietly. I think I hear my name once or twice, but I'm not totally sure.

All of a sudden Gram is knocking on my door. "Can I come in?" she's asking, smiling as if she already knows the answer. She pushes Beezer off the bed and brushes the fur from my sheets. "That dumb dog thinks he lives here."

"We're only watching him."

"Ha. I say he's moved in permanently." Finally she stops whacking my sheets and sits herself near my pillow. "I was so busy talking to your mom that I lost track of the time. And I hate to say it, but I do have a bus to catch."

I put down my book. "You mean now?"

"In a few." She takes my left hand and frowns. "You've let that go," she scolds.

"Let what?"

"The polish. I was looking at you all weekend, and I couldn't tell what was different. Now I realize. You're not wearing nail polish."

I shrug. "I did that with Emma."

"Well, you should keep it up, with or without Emma. Most of your colors are not my personal cup of tea, but sometimes it looks pretty snazzy."

When I don't answer that, Gram's face softens. "You know what, cookie? Things will get better. And I'm sure you'll get your friend back, if you don't give up."

"Gram," I say. "It's not about *me* giving up. *Emma's* the one who's too scared to be friends."

"Well, if you want my opinion, Emma could use a stiffer spine. Beezer, don't even *think* about jumping back on this bed." She wags her finger, but Beezer jumps on anyway.

I stroke his smelly head. He licks my nose.

Gram smiles. "Anyway," she says, "I've been doing a little thinking, Mari, and I might have an idea."

"You mean about Emma? *What?*"

"I shouldn't say. Just let me work on it a bit. And in the meantime, will you do something for me?"

"Sure!"

"Try to trust your mom a little." She kisses my forehead, then carefully smears off the magenta lipstick. "She's doing the best she can, you know? And you may not believe this, honey, but she understands you better than you think."

* * *

In homeroom on Monday, Mr. Hubley is handing out Spring After-school Sign-Ups. Amazingly, kids are flipping pages in the pamphlet, reading club names out loud, acting like they really care about this. Even Layla looks interested in her pamphlet, despite the fact that Jada's mom shot down her proposal, and called her parents over the weekend to inform them that jousting in middle school was "entirely inappropriate." (Layla told me about this as soon as I sat down; I could tell she was really proud.)

"Hey, Bananas!" Brody is shouting. "Check out page three. That's your mom, right?" He shoves his open pamphlet in my face, so I automatically push it away.

Then I open my own pamphlet. Yup, there she is.

DON'T JUST STAND THERE,
DO SOMETHING!

Calling all divas-in-hiding,
sit-down stand-ups, singers-in-the-shower, bit players, understudies,

drama geeks, and extras. Let's play! In this club we'll explore the games and techniques of theater improv, so you can learn to think on your feet, lose your inhibitions, command the stage, free your inner thespian. Mostly, though, we'll just act silly. Come as you are; no performing experience necessary. In fact, the less the better!!!

Becca Bailey is a nationally known performance artist and theater instructor. She has performed on and off stage all of her life.

Well, I think. *They've got that right.*

"Yo, Marigold, your mom's a performance artist?" Brody is asking.

"Yeah," I say. "What about it?"

"Nothing. I'm just curious. Does she do that thing where she's buried underwater? Or, wait, what was that thing I saw on TV? Oh yeah: This guy hung upside down in a park for, like, three days. Does she do stuff like that?"

Jada is looking at me. So are Megan and Ashley. So are Layla and Quinn, and a couple of girls from my gym class. Also Ethan; he's blushing slightly, or maybe it's just the weird fluorescent light in this room.

"No," I say firmly. "She doesn't."

Now Jada is doing her hyper-sympathetic smile. "Your mom does other things, though, right?"

"Like what?" Brody demands.

"Look her up on Wikipedia," Jada says helpfully. "There's a whole article."

She covers her mouth and says something to Ashley. Then Ashley whispers something in Megan's ear.

I'm suddenly aware of leaky eyebrows. Because I know exactly what's on Wikipedia; Beau and Bobbi cowrote an article last spring, complete with a bit from the "LICE" poem ("Itch. *Itch.* ITCH!") and photos of *Plastic Surgery*. And, of course, the total last thing I need right now is a homeroom that's researching Mom online.

"You don't believe everything on the Internet, do you?" I say, shrugging. "Because you know, half that stuff is wrong."

"Really?" Jada bats her eyelashes like Bambi. "Which half?"

Somebody sniggers. Megan leans over and says something to Ashley.

"Jada, shut up," Layla mutters.

"Did you say something?" Jada asks.

"You heard me."

"Could you repeat that? A little louder? Because you know, we're all so mesmerized by the sound of your voice."

Layla snarls, then sits on her boots and pretends to read her pamphlet. I try to catch her eye, but she's fascinated by CPR for Babysitters, apparently.

When the bell rings, I'm about to go to her, but first Ethan walks over to my desk.

"Hey, Marigold," he says. "Are you doing your mom's club?"

"Of course not," I answer immediately. "And neither are you, right?"

"Right," he says. "I'm doing lacrosse."

I take a normal breath.

"But I think Brody is," he adds.

"Are you serious? *Why?*"

Ethan shrugs.

"Can't you talk him out of it?"

"Brody?" He makes an *are-you-kidding-me?* face.

"Please try," I beg. *"Please."* And grab his arm.

Then we both realize that I'm grabbing his arm.

He blinks at me with marshmallow-free eyelashes. "Okay, later," he mumbles, and half runs out the door.

Omigod, I think. *What did I just do?*

And it gets even worse. Because when I look up, I realize Jada is gaping at me. As if she's seen the whole thing, including the arm-grab.

The look in her eyes is not hyper-sympathetic.

All morning long, everyone is talking about the clubs.

Five kids tell me they're signing up for Mom's, including two girls from my gym class.

In math, Ashley and Megan pass me a note. WE'RE TAKING YOUR MOM'S CLUB! 8D! When I look up at them, Ashley smiles. Which has to be ironic, because with everything Jada's been telling her about Mom, there's no way she's actually psyched about improv.

In health class, Brody leans over my desk. "Hey, Bananas," he says. "Was your mom ever chained to a rotating gyroscope?"

"Why are you asking?" I manage to say. "Was yours?"

Twice I catch Jada staring in my direction.

Not Ethan, though. He doesn't look at me at all. I think I freaked him out with the arm-grab, which I can't even blame on Mom. (Okay, well, maybe indirectly. But

I guess I could have begged him to talk to Brody without cutting off his circulation.)

And right outside the lunchroom, Mr. Shamsky waves me over. "Improv has a wait list," he says excitedly. "Your mom'll be so pleased."

"I'll tell her," I lie. Then I run into the lunchroom, grab a turkey sandwich, and plop next to Layla. "Where's everybody else?"

"Math retest. Although I think Ethan's afraid of you."

"Excuse me?"

"The way you attacked his arm? In homeroom?"

Ulp. "Did everyone see?"

"Probably. I mean, dude, it was *homeroom*." She points at my sandwich. "There's no peanut butter in that thing, is there?"

I shake my head.

She takes a big bite of my sandwich and chews thoughtfully. "Jada's madly in love with him, you know. So my guess is, as of this morning, you've shot straight to the top of her enemies list."

"But why?" I say weakly. "It had nothing to do with her."

"*Everything* has to do with Jada. According to Jada."

She wipes her mouth with my napkin. "So okay, then, what *did* it have to do with?"

"You really want to hear?"

She nods.

"My mom," I say.

"Your mom. Okay, Marigold, now you're making total sense."

I take a quick look around to make sure no one is listening. Then I lower my voice, just in case. "I was just asking Ethan to talk to Brody. To tell him not to take her club."

She raises one eyebrow. "How come?"

"Because she's crazy."

There. I said it. *Becca Bailey is a nutcase.*

Layla opens up my sandwich and takes out all the tomato. She closes it up again and takes another big bite. "Hey, listen," she says, chewing. "Everybody's mom goes a little crazy sometimes. You know what mine did? She got so sick of my dad watching his stupid plasma TV all the time that she sold it on eBay. Behind his back."

"I don't mean my mom *goes* crazy," I say. "I mean she *is* crazy. As in, you don't know what she'll do next. Especially onstage."

"Whoa." Now she's eating the tomato. "Cool."

"Yeah, cool when it's not *your* mom." I definitely didn't mean to get into all this, but for some strange reason my mouth keeps moving. "She promised me she'd behave herself, so I said fine, do the club. But that was before I thought anyone would sign up. And suddenly it's this huge thing, Mr. Shamsky says there's a wait list, and I'm scared she'll do something really, really humiliating."

Layla scrunches up her forehead. "Why would she? You said she promised."

"Because she loves a big audience. It's like, if a bunch of people are watching her, she just goes *off.* Sometimes I think if I walked onstage in the middle of one of her performances, she wouldn't even know who I was."

"That's kind of . . . intense."

"And if she *does* go off," I add, thinking out loud, "I won't even be there to know it."

Layla wipes her mouth with my napkin. "Well, anyway, you can relax about that part. I'm in the club, so I'll keep you totally informed."

I stare at her. "Wait. You're doing *Improv?*"

"So is Quinn. And you want to hear the best part? It was all her own idea. She said she thought it would help her *overcome her shyness*. Can you believe she actually said that?"

I shake my head hopelessly.

"And who knows." She drops her voice. "Maybe it'll help with my stage fright. I *hate* blanking out like a total moron. Remember that stupid ziti? I stood there like a *wall*."

"Layla," I say. "It's not going to help."

"Well, gee, Marigold, thanks for that vote of—"

"I just mean the whole club will be the Becca Bailey Freak Show. It's not going to be about you or Quinn or overcoming anything. It's just going to be about *her*."

She takes off her thumb ring and rolls it around in her palm a few times, like she's weighing it. Then she puts it back on. "Okay, you really want to know what I think? First of all, you should give your mom a chance. She promised you, and maybe she'll keep her promise. Or maybe not; she sounds like she doesn't have much of a track record."

"She doesn't."

"But if she *doesn't* keep her promise, and she goes a little Looney Tunes, at least I'll be there to let you know."

"Hey, leave Looney Tunes alone." I sigh. "Okay, fine. But what if I'd rather *not* know?"

"I thought you said—"

"Well, what if I change my mind?"

"You shouldn't," she insists. "Because if something weird happens, you don't want to be the last to hear. Not the way gossip spreads at this stupid school."

I groan. This isn't what I wanted from Layla; it's way too logical. But I think about Ashley and Megan signing up, and probably reporting everything back to Jada, and I can't really disagree with Layla's argument.

"And second of all," she continues, "why are you so worried about *me*? Or Quinn? Or Brody, even if he's in jerk mode? I mean, I don't know how to break the news to you, Marigold, but along with Ethan, whose elbow you're in love with, we're your *friends* around here."

"I know that," I murmur. "Thanks, Layla."

But I'm thinking: *Truthfully? That's exactly why I'm worried.*

Mine Shaft

The whole next week was spring break, but there's not much to tell. The major thing is that Dad drove to Lawson to fetch Kennedy and me and then drive us all the way back to his house. It was okay to be there for maybe the first afternoon, but after a while there was basically nothing to do besides eat Oreos and watch TV. So Kennedy and I went to Rite Aid and bought a whole bunch of pretend-vacation nail polish: *Spring Fling! Cherry Soda! Surf's Up!* And for the next three days I polished all our nails, first Kennedy's (including toenails), then mine.

She was thrilled. She kept saying her nails looked

"gorge." I don't know where she got that word from, but I was so relieved to hear her say something besides prairie-talk that I didn't bother pointing out that Laura Ingalls Wilder probably never polished her toenails.

On the fourth day Mona showed up at dinner, wearing a diamond engagement ring, which she referred to as "a rock."

"It's very nice," I said politely.

But Kennedy wasn't so polite. "Did you give a rock to Mom?" she asked Dad.

"Kennie," I said into my napkin.

"Your mom didn't want one," Dad answered, putting his arm around Mona's bony shoulders.

"Why not?" Kennedy pressed. "Did you offer to *buy* her one?"

I widened my eyes at her, but she wouldn't even look at me.

"She told me she thought engagement rings were too specific," Dad explained patiently. "And that when she's performing, she likes to be a blank slate."

"Isn't that something," Mona commented. "Imagine being so stagestruck that you don't even want one of these." She held out her French-manicured fingers (which was a nail polish look Emma and I both thought was kind of tacky) and wiggled her ring to make the diamond sparkle.

And the whole rest of the week I kept thinking about that word: "stagestruck." It sounded like a starry-eyed girl in an old-fashioned novel, and it made me wonder if that's how Mom was, way back in college when she first met Dad.

But it also sounded like "crazy," which brought it right up to the present.

It's the Monday after spring break. I'm sitting in Room 306, waiting for the start of Quilting Quorum, which is the club I finally signed up for. Okay: I know it sounds Jessamine the Prairie Girl, but it was either this or Beginners' Badminton, and I couldn't see myself whacking a little birdie back and forth, back and forth, every Monday through Friday afternoons for the next ten weeks. And when I found out that Beginners' Badminton was being coached by *Mr. Hubley*, well, let's just say that sealed the deal for Quilting Quorum.

So here I am. Me and three eighth-grade girls named Kirsten, Lexie, and Molly, plus the art teacher Ms. Canetti, who wears long, flowery skirts and is in love with my name. "Marigold," she repeats when she's taking attendance. "What an absolutely beautiful word. It reminds me of—"

"Marigolds?" Kirsten suggests, and Molly and Lexie start to snicker.

Ms. Canetti looks at them with teacher-eyes. Then she looks at me and smiles. "Springtime," she finishes. "Are you named after someone?"

"No. I think my mom just liked it."

"Well, she has excellent taste. *Marigold*. It almost sounds like a nineteenth-century quilter, doesn't it? Can't you imagine a lovely young woman—"

I'm just about to drown in eyebrow-sweat when the door bursts open.

Jada.

"Sorry I'm late," she tells Ms. Canetti breathlessly. "I was helping my mom. She's running after-school and the gym was locked, so she asked me to find the janitor—" Then she notices me. Her face freezes over.

"No problem, Jada," Ms. Canetti says cheerfully. "We're just getting started. Take a seat anywhere."

Jada sits herself next to Kirsten, in the seat as far from me as possible. As if I totally don't exist, but even so, I might have some deadly virus. I notice Kirsten look over at Molly and Lexie whispering.

Then Ms. Canetti starts passing around some quilt-ing books "for inspiration," she says. I'm flipping pages, listening to her talk about patterns with scary-sounding titles like Blue Winter and Hidden Wells and Mine Shaft, and I'm thinking: *What did I get myself into? This is totally not me.*

Plus Jada is in this club, and she's giving me the evil eye.

Maybe there's room in Origami. Or in CPR for Babysitters. Or in anything but this. This and Improv.

Ms. Canetti starts talking about some projects we'll be doing, which don't sound a bit like alien mutant ten-tacled Things. She says we can bring fabric from home, or she'll supply some of her own "if we'd prefer." (When she asks for a show of hands, I shoot mine straight up for Ms. Canetti's supply.) And when she tells us we're through for the day, even though it's early, I skid out the door as if I'm wearing poofy bedroom slippers.

On the way out I pass the auditorium, which is where Improv meets. I'm hoping to catch up with Layla so she can snitch about Day 1. But the auditorium is locked, and there's a sign duct-taped to the doors, writ-ten in one of Mom's jumpy computer fonts: PLEASE KEEP CLOSED!!! ACTORS AT PLAY.

I stand there for a minute, trying to eavesdrop.

The first thing I hear is a piercing scream. Then a loud crash, and furniture squeaking. Then a bunch of people laughing hysterically.

Then two piercing screams.

Then more crashing, and more hysterical laughs.

My stomach knots up.

Because whatever "game" Mom has them "playing," I can tell it's completely insane.

And there's nothing I can do to stop it.

At dinner Mom is ecstatic.

"The club went GREAT," she announces as she takes a big slurp of lentil curry. "All the kids were amazingly motivated. Plenty of tightness initially, but by the end, juices were definitely flowing. You could see it in their eyes."

"See what?" I mutter. "Juices?"

"Don't be gross at the table, precious daughter." She laughs. "Marigold, I really don't understand why you were so down on my club. Your classmates are just terrific. Do you know some girls named Ashley and Megan?"

"Yes, but they're not my friends." Then I shut myself up.

Kennedy is watching my face with sharp eyes. When I look back at her, she turns away. "So what games did you play?" she asks Mom. I see her sneak a piece of bread to Beezer, who's sniffing around under the table.

"Oh, lots," Mom answers brightly. "Let's see. First we did some stretching and breathing in the rehearsal room, and I introduced 'Yes, And'—"

"What's that?" Kennedy asks, dropping some bread crust on my foot.

"I never explained 'Yes, And' to you? Really?" Mom shakes her head, as if she can't believe she's been so negligent in Kennedy's upbringing. "It's *only* the basic law of improv: When one actor has an idea, the other actors need to accept that idea and build on it. So whenever your scene-partner comes up with something, you're always supposed to be saying '*Yes, and* also that.' Like if I say to you, 'Hey, did you have a nice vacation?' you say something back like, 'Yes, I did, and when I got home, I could speak five new languages.' That's how two actors advance a scene."

"Oh," Kennedy says, feeling around under the table for Beezer, and grabbing my knee instead.

"OW," I complain. Kennedy gives me an innocent blink.

Mom ignores me. "*Any*way. So then we did some 'Yes, And' games; the one they liked best was Emotional Mirror, where they had to pass feelings back and forth while they were talking about the weather. Then we did Scream, which is the one where you make a big circle, and whenever two people make eye contact, they scream as loud as they can and drop dead."

"Sounds fun," I say. "And do they crash into furniture?"

"Of course not," Mom replies, laughing. "Sometimes they get what we call *furniture bites*, but it's never a big deal. Oh, and at the end I tried Big Blob, where you set up a scene—it could be about anything—but you tell the players that there's an enormous blob in the room that they have to walk around, or go through, or deal with somehow. But the trick is, they can't talk about it. It was extremely challenging, probably way too advanced for the first day, but I think we were really starting to get the hang—"

The phone rings.

"I'll get it," Kennedy says eagerly.

"Ignore it, Kennie," Mom orders. She waves her hand toward the phone. "People should respect the dinner hour."

"It's not the dinner hour, it's eight o'clock," I point out. I go into the kitchenette and answer the phone. "Hello?"

"Yeah." Then there's silence. "Um, hi. Is this . . . Marigold?"

My heart flips. "Ethan?"

"Right. I didn't have your cell, so I called Information."

"Oh, that's fine. We're not eating dinner."

"I thought. So, yeah, I tried to talk to Brody."

I lower my voice. "You mean about the club?"

"Yeah."

Nothing. Total dead silence.

"And what happened?" I ask.

"He's doing it. He said it's awesome."

"*Why?*"

"I don't know. He likes your mom."

"Okay, well, thanks for trying." I peek out the kitchenette; Mom and Kennedy are chatting away. "So how was lacrosse?"

"Pretty decent. You're in . . . ?"

"Quilting Quorum. But I'm probably switching out."

"How come?"

"It's not really . . . what I do."

"Well, give it a few days. Who knows, maybe you'll like it."

Ethan is so smart, I think. *And so nice. And his voice sounds sooo incredibly cute on the phone.*

I really, really wish I could call Emma.

"Well, anyway," he says. "I wanted to tell you about Brody."

All right, so now what do I say? I've already thanked him. *Improvise,* I tell myself. *Advance the scene.* "Maybe we can walk home tomorrow," I blurt out.

"Okay," he says. "Yeah, cool."

I do a mime-scream. *He said okay. He said COOL.*

Then he coughs. "Uh, can I say something?"

"Sure!"

"You probably shouldn't tell anybody."

"About what? That we're walking home together?"

"Yeah. I know it sounds stupid. But Jada's so paranoid. And if she hears . . ."

"What could she do?"

He doesn't answer.

"You know what?" I say with pretend-bravery. "She's just this *person.* I'm not afraid of her. I even feel sorry for her."

"Okay, that's stupid."

"Yeah, maybe," I admit. "But she's not some evil villain, right? So why should we let her scare us?"

"She's not scaring *me*," he answers. "I told you before, she *likes* me. That's kind of the problem."

"So if she likes you—"

"Hey, it's not me I'm worried about, Marigold. It's you."

Snickers

By the time I get off the phone, Mom is off doing Evening Walk, which I decide is really lucky. Because who knows what my face looks like right now, but my guess is mostly ecstatic with a subtle hint of freaked-out, and I don't need Mom playing Read Marigold's Expression. I don't need Kennedy playing it either, so instead of doing my homework at my desk while she reads *Louisa's New Bonnet* or whatever American Dreams book she's probably memorizing at the moment, I hang out in the kitchenette with Beezer and listen to him snore like an old man on a bus.

Next morning after breakfast Mom informs me

that since her newest Morning Walker, a mutt named Snickers, lives across the street from my school, she and Beezer and Darla will "keep me company" on the walk over.

"You don't have to," I tell her with a mouth full of toothpaste.

"I know I don't *have* to, but I *want* to," she replies firmly.

Once Kennedy is on her bus and we pick up Darla, who immediately pees all over a fire hydrant, Mom says, "So. Was that Dad who called at supper last night?"

I shake my head.

"Anyone I know?"

"Just a kid from school. And no, he's not in your club."

"That wasn't what I meant." Mom tugs on the earflaps of her hat, and winds both leashes around her mittens. We walk for a couple of blocks, and then suddenly she blurts out, "So listen, Mari, there's something I wanted to say to you. I had some good long talks with Gram over the weekend, and I've been doing a lot of personal soul-searching—"

Here we go, I think.

"And I've decided I'm fine about Dad's wedding. I

mean, life goes on, right? And if he wants to waste his with Mona, who am I to stop him?"

"You really mean that?" I ask doubtfully. Because the truth is, ever since Dad broke the news, I've been half expecting the world premiere of *Nu-Mona, Second Wife of Doom*.

"Yes, baby, I really do," she insists. "And good luck to them both!"

We keep walking, not talking, trying to keep Darla from peeing on every other mailbox. Beezer poops on somebody's front lawn, then looks at us like, *Whoa, you see that?*

Mom pretends she doesn't. "And while we're on the subject," she adds, even though actually I thought we'd finished. "About this dude ranch business. I know it sounds awful—"

"It does," I interrupt. "I *really* don't want to go."

"Neither does Kennie. But you *should* go, both of you. For Dad. And also for what's-her-name."

"The Horrible Mona Woman," I say, and we both laugh.

"Guess I'll have to stop calling her that," she admits. "Maybe we can think up another name."

"I know. How about Mona the Human Being?"

"Naah, too generic. What about Mona Who Stole My Ex-Husband?"

"Too long," I insist. "Besides, she didn't, technically."

"Yeah, I suppose." She sighs a puff cloud. "The Horrible Mona Woman was perfect, wasn't it? Oh, well." She puts her arm around my shoulders. "You know what, Mari? I really cherish these mother-daughter chats."

I turn my head to see if she's smiling ironically, but she isn't. In fact, if I had to describe her expression, I'd say it was dreamy, maybe a bit like that stagestruck college girl I imagined at Dad's. And I know, I should probably say something back right then, some sort of "Yes, And" remark that *advances the scene*, or whatever improv-thing you're supposed to do.

But I'm drawing a total blank. Because it's like we were in the middle of one kind of scene, improvising lines back and forth, and then whammo: Out of nowhere, Mom changes the whole mood. Are you even allowed to do that? It seems kind of unfair.

Plus I told you about her dramatic timing, right? So like the *very second* she says her line about the mother-daughter chats, the dogs yank us in front of school. And now Beezer is lurching toward his flagpole, the bus doors are opening, kids are crashing into us, and Layla is running over, one arm waving like a windshield wiper. "Marigold!" she's shouting. "Stop!"

By the time she catches up to us, her cheeks are clashing with the bright orange streak in her hair. "Sorry," she says, gasping. "I didn't think you heard me! Cute doggies."

"They're not ours," I say automatically.

She isn't listening, though. Or even looking at the dogs. She's just grinning stupidly at Mom.

"Layla, right?" Mom says, beaming right back at her. "You did so well yesterday."

"I did?"

"Oh, definitely. You were a little tight when we first started, but I loved your Scream with that boy."

Layla giggles. "You mean Brody."

"Right, Brody. You two had excellent eye contact."

"You think so? Seriously? Because he's such a jerk."

"Let me tell you something," Mom says. "In theater, chemistry is very mysterious. That's one of the few things actors never overanalyze."

I'm just about to say, *Okay, well, time to shove off, Mom, see you around,* and also yank Layla into the building, when who should be heading toward us but Ashley and Megan.

Oh, perfect. Jada's hench-girls.

"Becca!" Ashley is calling. "Becca!"

"Wow, look, more of my kids," Mom exclaims happily, waving them over.

Her kids? I try to catch Layla's eye, but she's staring at her pointy black boots like they're the most fascinating footwear ever invented.

So now here we all are right outside Crampton Middle School: me, Mom, two dogs who don't belong to us, Layla with her fascinating boots, plus Jada's not-so-secret agents, both of them standing too close and gushing about how *fabulous* the club was yesterday, how they *loved* doing the Blob thing, how great it felt to scream like that, and could Mom *please* tell them what she's planned for today, they promise not to tell anybody, they just can't *wait.*

"If I told you, it wouldn't be improv, would it?" Mom answers, laughing.

Ashley does a pseudo-pout. "Oh, but Becca—"

"Remember what I said yesterday? The key to acting is surprise. If I don't surprise you, why should you even watch me?"

Okay, that's it. We are SO not talking about Mom's talent for surprises.

Especially because at this exact moment I see Jada

getting off a bus. When she steps onto the sidewalk, she looks around, like she's wondering what happened to her welcome party.

Then she spots us. She stands there, her arms on her hips, her red scarf snapping in the wind. And maybe I'm right, maybe she's not some evil villain, but right now she definitely resembles one.

"Uh, Mom?" I say loudly. "Don't you have to go get Snickers?"

Ashley grins. "Snickers? We're having *chocolate* today, Becca?"

"NO," I blurt. "Snickers is a dog. Mom walks them. As a job."

"That is so, so cool," Megan exclaims.

"Yes, it is," Mom says, lovingly patting Darla's head. "Really, I get my best inspirations walking my canine buddies. Some people think in the shower, but I personally—"

"And you don't want to be late," I insist, staring at Mom.

Mom stares right back at me. "Late?"

"For your walk. With Snickers."

Ashley laughs. "I'm sure Snickers doesn't have an alarm clock, Marigold."

"Oh, but he's very hyper about his schedule," I say. "And if Mom's five minutes late, he goes totally bonkers."

Now everyone is staring at me.

"You should hear him bark," I add desperately. "It's like . . ." *Ack, what's it like?* "You know, dog barking. Loud."

Layla starts coughing into her glove. And I'm sure she's probably thinking I sounded insane just now, but I had to do something. Because Jada is definitely walking in our direction. And this whole scene is excruciating enough without Jada joining in, telling Layla she can't hear her, and asking Mom about Wikipedia.

Mom gives me a look like, *Remind me to teach you some social skills, Marigold.* But she doesn't argue. She flashes me a quick smile, kisses my cheek, and to everybody else calls out, "Okay, see you later, guys." Then she walks off with the dogs, giving Beezer one sharp tug before he pees on the school flagpole.

Don't Mind Me

The whole next week is pretty much torture.

All I hear at school is how amazing Mom is, how creative, how fun, how you-fill-in-the-blank-with-your-complimentary-adjective. After all the time I've spent listening to people gossip about her and snigger, you'd think I'd be relieved to hear what an idol she's become, but I'm not. The truth is, I'm terrified that any minute some kid is going to drink canola oil, and then we'll all be drowning in free negative publicity. And even though Layla keeps telling me that (so far) Mom hasn't done anything "too Looney Tunes," I'm not sure Layla's concept of crazy is the universal standard.

Plus it just feels funny to have everyone—I mean, like, the *entire school*—start worshipping your mother. Even kids I barely know are coming up to me all the time, going, "Oh, Marigold, your mom is sooo cool," and "Hey, Marigold, tell your mom I said hi!" I'm starting to feel not like Marigold but like Becca Bailey's Daughter, and to be perfectly honest, it's starting to get a bit annoying.

Take, for example, right this minute in the lunchroom.

I'm sitting across from Ethan, who is wearing a faded green sweatshirt that makes his freckles stand out. Every once in a while he glances at me, but our rule is Keep It Secret for Now, so we're careful to avoid eye contact.

"Meep!" Layla is saying. She sniffs Quinn's Tupperware. "Wazza drogool?"

"Plah-koo," Quinn answers. She hands Layla some chopsticks. "Spinky."

Layla grins. "Na na, dweepy bobo." She twirls some noodles around her chopsticks, then dangles them in the air. "Yoppy kerploova fablum! Poogy yackum."

The noodles drip. Plop, plop, plop. Probably tamari sauce.

"Pek. Fazzle reeka," Quinn scolds, wiping the table with a napkin.

Ethan puts down his burrito. "Okay, sorry to interrupt, but are you talking English today?"

"They can't," Brody informs him. "It's homework. For Becca."

"Jaddo," Layla adds, with a mouthful of noodles. "Pizzy alla fadoo drep."

"Yeah," Ethan grumbles, glancing at me through his eyelashes. "So you're going to do this *again*? For, like, the entire *lunch* period?"

"Jez," Brody tells him, nodding very seriously. "Veezer."

Quinn starts laughing so hard some water leaks out of her mouth. Layla hands her back the saucy napkin, then leans over and messes Brody's hair. He grins at her and says something that sounds like *aardvark painkiller*.

"Okay, this is getting too strange." Ethan stands. "Later," he adds, I'm pretty sure to me, and walks off to sit with some jocks from the lacrosse team.

Layla winces. "Sorry."

"For what?" I ask innocently.

She cocks her head like, *Don't act so innocent.*

"Marigold?" Quinn says. "Do you want to do Becca's exercise with us? It's really fun."

"Oh, no thanks!" I answer. "We talk gibberish at home all the time."

Brody's eyes light up. "You do?"

"I think that was a joke, you moron," Layla says. She looks at me. "So it's okay with you if we—?"

"Yup. Don't mind me."

She shrugs. "Okay, then, if you insist. Verspeezle fregony karple plunkert—"

And on they go with the alien-talk. Which leaves me nothing to do but nibble my lunch, a soggy ham-and-cheddar-and-bruised-lettuce-on-cardboard-pita. Too bad I didn't bring a book; even *The Lord of the Rings* would be better than sitting here listening to nonsense syllables for the third day in a row. But at least I can use the free brain-time to space about Ethan—the way we held hands for a full block yesterday on the walk home, until we ran into Brody's mother. ("And who is *this*?" she asked Ethan, smiling suspiciously at me as if I was maybe something he shoplifted.)

This makes me think about Emma, how great it would be to share every detail with her, exactly how we used to talk about Will and Matt. But since that last phone conversation, she hasn't tried to contact me. Not once, not even a borrowed-cell-phone voice mail *Hey, what's up, bye* sort of deal. I have a terrible thought then: Maybe the "break" Emma talked about isn't only "until things settle down" at her house. Maybe "things" are permanently broken, and they're never going to be fixed.

Unless Gram's made any progress with her plan, whatever it is. She hasn't said a word about it since her visit, though. Probably that means there's nothing to report. Because I'm sure she would call me the second there was any news.

"Hey, okay if we join you?"

My eyes refocus: It's Ashley and Megan. *Ashley and Megan?*

"Join us for what?" Layla asks, not too nicely either.

"Improv homework," Ashley says, shrugging. "The gibberish thing."

Layla raises her eyebrow at Quinn, who nods a little reluctantly, but she does nod. "Dro," Layla says, moving closer to Brody. And now there's a space at the table big enough for Ashley and Megan to squeeze in, especially because Megan is half the width of dental floss.

Okay, well, this is certainly bizarre.

"Prissky," Megan murmurs politely.

"Prissky," Ashley echoes, just as polite. "Speena kiff oodwee pennygrapple hooble—"

This goes on for a few demented minutes. You can tell everyone feels incredibly awkward about the seating arrangement, but even so, they're all fake-talking, back and forth, and no one is giving the evil eye or throwing pasta or bursting into tears. It's really kind of amazing, actually.

But then suddenly they all stop. Total frozen silence. Because here comes Jada, her hands on her hips.

"What are you doing?" she asks in a fakely super-calm voice.

Ashley's face turns bright pink. "A theater exercise. Becca wants us to practice gibberish with as many partners as possible."

"Gibberish? You're joking, right?"

"She says talking in gibberish frees your imagination. And teaches you to listen better."

Jada rolls her eyes. "So she's making you talk *baby talk*. And for partners you picked these—"

"We had to," Megan mutters, looking at the table. "It's not like we *chose* to sit here."

"Yeah, well, that's obvious. Anyway, you guys have to do this right *now*?"

"Kind of," Megan says. "Becca wants us to talk about food. That's the assignment."

Jada sighs deeply. "So how much longer is this going to take?"

"Five minutes. Maybe ten."

"Lunch is *over* in ten minutes."

"Jada, this is our homework," Ashley says. Now her ears are hot pink. "We really need to do this. Becca says—"

"Fine," Jada interrupts. "Do this." Her eyes dart around the table. "So anyway, where's Ethan?"

"Squeep," I blurt out.

Everyone stares at me.

"Squeep," I repeat, louder this time.

Quinn starts giggling.

Layla grins. "Squeep," she says, nodding. "Squeep."

"Yez, squeep," Brody says. "Squeepsqueepsqueep—"

"Stop that," Jada says sharply. "It's moronic, even for you, Brody." She glares at Ashley and Megan. "Well? Is someone going to answer me in English?"

"Squeep," Layla insists. "Fazoo wobby farple."

"Fazoo wobby treeny," Quinn replies. "Gopper."

"Shut up," Jada snaps. "All of you. You're acting like total jerks, you know that?"

Then she storms off.

* * *

That afternoon in Quilting Quorum, Ms. Canetti is swishing her flowery skirt around the room, watching us lay out our patterns and offering comments like, "Ooh, I'm in love with your focal fabric," and "Try not to make it too matchy matchy." When she gets to my desk, she stops. "Oh, Marigold," she says, noticing the fabric bits scattered all over my desk. "You haven't gotten very far, have you?"

"I'm still deciding what to do."

"You mean you haven't chosen a pattern yet? Just pick any one. I showed you those books—"

"I'm not sure I want to make a pattern," I confess. "I'm not even sure I want to make a quilt."

Ms. Canetti does the kind of smile you do when you don't know what to say. "Let's think about this," she murmurs. Then she swishes over to the eighth graders, Kirsten, Lexie, and Molly, who are sitting in a private group with their backs to Jada.

Jada looks up at me like she can feel my eyes on her. She stands and walks over to me, casually, then leans over my desk so I can smell her shampoo. Or maybe it's perfume; there's an extra wave of something flowery that you don't get just from washing your hair.

"Nice fabric," she says quietly. "I like your colors."

She's complimenting me? After I started the "squeep" business at lunch? "Thanks," I say uneasily.

She does a quick no-tooth smile. "Does Becca like to quilt?"

"My mom? Oh, no. She can't even thread a needle."

"That's so funny." She picks up a scrap, a neon-green satin bit that Ms. Canetti had cut into a perfect square. "Because doesn't she make her own costumes?"

"Not really. Well, she *makes* them, but she doesn't *sew* them."

"I guess she uses other material? Didn't she make one out of aluminum foil?"

"Saran Wrap."

"Right. I saw that photo on Wikipedia."

I'm suddenly aware of my eyebrows. "That's not all she does."

"Oh, I *know*. I've been reading about her online. And also Ashley and Megan won't shut up about her. They say she's really wild."

"Actually," I say, "I'm pretty sure they like her."

"Oh, they do! Because she's so entertaining. I mean she'll just do *anything*, right? All the other moms—" She shrugs.

"What?"

"Well, you know they're not like that. My mom is always going, *Wow, that Becca Bailey is something. And she has such strong opinions!* And omigod, I hear my mom on the phone with Brody's . . . Well, you know how they talk. I try to tune her out, but it's impossible." She sighs. "Anyway, Marigold, you're so incredibly lucky. Everyone else's parents are so *normal*."

"Uh, thanks."

"But sometimes aren't you a little . . . I don't know. Uncomfortable?"

"No," I say quickly. "Why should I be?"

Jada fixes me with her hyper-sympathetic eyes. She doesn't answer my question; she just lets it dangle in the air, the way Layla dangles noodles.

"Anyhow," she says finally, "you just seem totally different."

I swallow. My throat feels vacuumed-out, like I just ate ten peppermints.

"What I mean," she explains, leaning closer, "is I can tell you're a sensitive person. You really care what other people think. And what they say behind your back." She slides the green square across my desk. "That's how I am, incredibly sensitive. It makes things hard, though, doesn't it? Because people can be so nasty."

Okay, I'm starting to lose it now. "Jada," I say, hearing my voice wobble. "If you're trying to say something, just say it."

She does the Bambi-blink. "You're sure?"

I nod once.

"Okay, then." She cups her hand around my ear. When she speaks, her hot breath fills up my head. "Everyone says you're trying to steal Ethan from me. But I know you wouldn't do anything so tacky, or anything people would *say* was tacky. Because you're already so freaked by all the talk about your mom."

She touches my arm, like she's afraid I'll break. "Did I upset you, Marigold? I'm really so, so sorry."

The Deep End

As soon as Quilting Quorum is over, I grab my stuff and run.

I don't want to see Ethan or Layla or anybody else. I don't want people saying to me, *Oh, Marigold, Jada's horrible. She's worse than horrible; she's evil. Whatever she says to you, think the opposite.*

And I don't even want people saying, *Oh, Marigold, your mom is awesome. Jada's jealous; just ignore her.*

Because I can't. One thing I know for sure right now: This isn't about Jada Sperry. This isn't even about Ethan and me. This is about Becca Bailey, because it's *always* about Becca Bailey. And I can't let her keep hurling my life into total chaos.

When I get home, she's not there yet, of course; she's still at Improv. But Kennedy is there, her bare feet up on the coffee table. And this other person, a small, pointy-faced girl, is polishing Kennedy's nails. With my nail polish.

"This color is soooo gorge," the pointy-faced girl is saying. "What's it called again?"

"Fun in the Sun," Kennedy answers. "Watch it, you're dripping some on my foot."

"Hello?" I call out.

Kennedy jumps up. "Oh, Mari! Hi! This is Dexter. She asked if we could borrow your polish. I said it was okay, because you never use it, right?"

"Right. Though you should have asked first." Wasn't Dexter the mean girl who called Kennie a spaz in gym? I look at my sister, her eyes huge and pleading behind her glasses. "Actually," I say, "this color doesn't work for me. You want it?"

Kennie throws her arms around me. "Thanks, Mari," she murmurs.

"Wow, Ken, your sister's soooo cool," Dexter says, her beady little eyes popping.

That's when the front door opens, and Mom bursts into the living room in her purple Wagley College sweats, her cheeks glowing, her hair all sproingy. "Sorry I'm late," she says, panting. "I tried to end the club early, but they just wouldn't leave. Is this Dexter?"

"I'm really glad to meet you, Mrs. Bailey," Dexter says shyly. "Kennedy's been telling me about you."

Mom beams, as if Dexter is now officially one of *her kids*. "Call me Becca," she says, and plops onto the sofa.

For the next hour and a half, I'm in my room, listening through the walls to Mom chatting up Dexter, and Dexter giggling hysterically, and then the doorbell. "Bye!" Mom sings out. "We'll have Dexter over for dinner next time!" I wait a few minutes for the Chocolate Night DVD to stop playing in my head. Then I go to the kitchenette, where Beezer is noisily chomping his kibble and Mom is pulling stuff out of the pantry.

As soon as she sees me, she dumps some peanut butter into a mixing bowl. "What a successful day," she announces. "Kennie's made a nice friend, we had a truly *spectacular* Improv, I think I've just had an inspiration for a new piece, and this morning I got Bob's approval for the Mochahouse." She drizzles some honey into the bowl, frowns, then drizzles some more. "What's up with you, baby?"

"Nothing," I sputter. *"Mochahouse?"*

"Cutesy name, right?" She laughs. "Apparently every June all the clubs have an open house for the parents. And I had this idea for an Improv coffeehouse, so my kids could perform in front of a live audience. But Lisa Sperry is making us call it a Mochahouse, because, as she puts it, *"Coffee is inappropriate for middle schoolers."* I swear, that woman is driving me completely—"

Your cue, Marigold. "You're not fighting with her, are you?"

"Well, I'm expressing contrary viewpoints. But don't worry, always in an *appropriate* manner." She rips open a bag of sunflower seeds and pours the entire contents into the bowl. Now she's chopping apples. "Why do you ask?"

"I don't know. I heard some stuff today."

"Oh, really?" Chop, chop, chop. "What sort of stuff?"

"About you."

"Ah, free publicity. The best kind." She stirs the goopy mixture with a spatula, frowns, then adds some raisins. "And who said this newsworthy stuff?"

"Some girl I know. She's not in your club."

"So apparently word travels. Well, that's good to hear." She takes the spatula and smears the goop all over her arm.

"Mom? Uh, what are you doing?"

"Research." She holds out her goopy arm and jiggles it slightly, like it's a branch fluttering in the wind. "I need to see if it's the right consistency. Hmm. Maybe a bit too thin. See how it's dripping off?"

"Okay," I say. "You know what? You've finally gone off the deep end."

"Oh, Mari, relax, it's for my new piece." She adds peanut butter to the bowl, then tastes the goop with her finger. "I'm calling it *Birdfeeder*. I'm going to stand in the park on Earth Day, smear this stuff all over my scuba gear, and see what happens. Maybe you can take some photos?"

I don't even answer that. I watch her add more raisins to her arm. "Mom, how can you keep doing this to us?"

"Doing this to *you*?" She spreads more goop. "This has nothing to do with you, baby. This is my work."

"I know it is! But you promised me—"

"I promised to keep my work separate from the

Improv Club. I never said I'd stop doing performances."

She has a point, doesn't she? Technically that's what she said. "But people will see," I argue lamely.

"They're *supposed* to see. That's the idea: to show people how we're one with nature. Or should be." She does three or four jumping jacks. Only a few raisins and some sunflower seeds fall off. "Maybe I should add some butter. Although, wait a sec: Do birds even like butter?"

Okay, just pretend she didn't ask that. "Mom. You're not advertising this *Birdfeeder* thing in the club, are you? Or talking about, I don't know, *Nu-Trisha*, or any other performance you've ever—"

"Marigold," Mom says, rinsing off her hands. "Enough already, okay? I'm getting tired of all these questions."

She didn't answer you! "So you're saying you *swear* you haven't—"

"Just stop it, all right?" She shakes her hands impatiently, spraying water on Beezer's head. "I really wish you'd listen to me!"

"I *am* listening. I'm totally listening. But this girl said—"

"Yes?" Her eyes are glowing now. Challenging me.

"That people are talking about you. They're reading about you online. And you haven't even *done* this stupid *Birdfeeder* act yet."

She crosses her still-goopy arms. "And that's what you're listening to? Not to your own mother, but to anonymous gossip? Fed to you by an unnamed girl? Wow, you're really hurting me, Marigold."

"No, Mom," I croak, "you're hurting *me*. You're doing exactly what you always do, and it's hurting *our whole family*."

Her face goes scary-pale, like she's just become a ghost of herself. I see her take a slow, deep yoga breath, then another. She rests her hands on my shoulders; I can feel damp fingerprints ruining my wool sweater, but I don't say anything else. I can't.

Finally she speaks in a quiet, choky voice. "I love you, Marigold. I wish you were prouder of my work, I wish you trusted me more, I wish you would forgive me about Emma. I can apologize to you until I'm blue in the face, but I can't control your feelings, and ultimately those things are your personal choice. All I ask is that when you judge me, you look at me with your own eyes. All right? Will you try to do that for me, please?"

Yes, And

For dinner Mom microwaves some veggie lasagna, but instead of eating with us, she takes Beezer out for an extra-long Evening Walk. The next morning she takes him while I'm still in the shower, so we never have one of those awkward post-fight meals, the kind where you don't know what to look at, and everyone is super-polite. Luckily, Kennedy is still ecstatic about Dexter, so she chatters away as if everything is normal.

In homeroom I apologize to Ethan for running out on him yesterday. "Girl emergency," I lie.

He definitely blushes. "What about today?"

"I can't. Tomorrow," I promise hurriedly, as Jada walks into the room.

All day long I keep thinking about Mom, how she asked me to look at her with my own eyes. *Well, sure,* I think. *Whose eyes does she expect me to look with?* But I have a sick feeling in my stomach that won't go away. It's as if, okay, I had it out with her, I needed to do it and good for me. But something went wrong. I'm not sure what, but I think I said something I can't take back this time. Layla and Quinn keep asking me if I'm okay, and I keep telling them I'm fine, but the truth is, I'm not. Not even close.

Right before dismissal I ask Layla to prop open the auditorium door.

"What for?" she asks suspiciously.

"No reason," I answer. "Will you?"

"Sure, why not. I do random stupid things all the time."

When the bell rings, I hang out in the wheelchair stall in the girls' room. A bunch of girls bang through; I recognize Ashley's laugh and Layla's boots, and also Kirsten, Lexie, and Molly from Quilting Quorum. When I'm sure everybody's gone, I come out of the stall and wash my hands.

For a long time then I study my face in the mirror: I'm pale right now, maybe because I didn't sleep last night, and today I didn't eat much lunch. But my hair looks pretty good: Dad's hair, luckily, not the sproingy stuff that Mom has. Although I definitely have her eyes: big, dark, and emotional. Maybe too emotional, sometimes. Exactly like hers.

I have a crazy thought then: If I look at the world through these eyes, am I looking through *her* eyes? No; of course not, I'm looking through my own. My eyes may *look* like hers, but they *see* things differently. Totally differently. I mean, we're totally different people.

But how do you *know* you're seeing things through your own eyes? Maybe you think you are, but really, you're just collecting other people's points of view. Maybe you're seeing the world through their eyes, and you don't even know it.

I wonder about that.

Because it's possible, isn't it, that I'm seeing Mom through Jada's eyes. And Lisa Sperry's. And everybody's since second grade, including Trisha Hartley and Emma. And even Gram and Kennedy and Dad and Mona; maybe I'm looking at her through their eyes too.

And maybe that's unfair to Mom. Maybe it's even unfair to me.

I drown my face in freezing water, then crank out some paper towel.

A couple of minutes later, I sneak into the auditorium. Layla had stuck a science textbook in the door, so I slip in easily. I crouch behind the sound-and-light board until I'm sure there's enough commotion onstage to distract everybody. When Mom tells everyone to start moving chairs around, I slide into a seat in the last row, slumped low enough so that only my eyes are showing over the row ahead of me.

Mom is scurrying around the stage in her bare feet, dressed in a black leotard I recognize from the chocolate cake performance. She's pointing where chairs ought to go, dragging some herself, chatting and smiling the whole time. "Okay," she's saying in her clear, strong theater voice. "We're working on Showing, not Telling. Remember, don't just talk *at* each other. Give and take, listen with your *entire body*, and *be specific*. Yes?"

Quinn is asking her a question. Mom puts her hand on Quinn's shoulder and nods enthusiastically. Quinn beams.

"Are we ready, then?" Mom calls out. "Okay, I've already paired you up, so let's get started with the Who Game. Remember, A knows the relationship, B doesn't. Curtain."

Then one after the other, kids get up onstage in twos, doing scenes about job interviews and surprise birthday parties and first dates. In every scene there's a moment when the A character tells the B character he knows her from somewhere else, and the B character goes, *Ohhhh*. Some of the kids seem nervous, like they have no idea what to say next, so Mom calls out little pep talks from the audience, like, "Keep it simple," and "Nothing is a mistake." A few of the kids (Brody, weirdly enough, and Megan) look perfectly comfortable walking around the stage and making up dialogue. And even though nothing they say is fascinating or hilarious, they almost seem like characters you'd watch in a real play.

Then Quinn gets up with this pudgy eighth-grade boy named Aaron. As soon as Quinn starts talking, Ashley calls out from the front row, "Hello? We can't hear you."

"Try to project," Mom says to Quinn.

Quinn nods. Her next line, though, is almost just as soft.

"Becca, I still can't hear anything," Ashley announces.

"Maybe you would if you stopped criticizing," Layla snaps.

"I'm not criticizing, I'm giving feedback. There's a difference. And Layla? You should actually mind your own business."

"Girls, that's enough." Mom jumps up onstage and talks privately to Quinn. I can tell by the way she's throwing back her own shoulders that she's correcting Quinn's posture. Finally Quinn takes a bunch of yoga breaths, straightens her back, and speaks. You still can't hear every word she's saying, but she's definitely louder.

When they finish the scene, Mom tells them she liked how specific they were, but how they need to "use the silence," whatever that means. Then she calls out, "Next pair," and Layla and Ashley take their places.

Uh-oh. Maybe, according to Mom, chemistry is mysterious, but right away you can tell this chemistry is just bad. Layla immediately curls herself up in a chair, while Ashley stands off to the side, her hands on her hips, glaring at her.

"Curtain," Mom says.

Layla stretches her legs. "God, I'm so bored," she

says. "Just sitting here, all by myself. I wish something would happen for once."

"Show, don't tell," Mom coaches. "Remember?"

Layla yawns.

"Better," Mom says.

Ashley saunters onstage. She points to an empty chair next to Layla. "Excuse me, is this seat taken?" she asks.

"What seat?" Layla snarls, looking around. "I don't see any seat."

Ashley purses her lips. "Oh, I guess you forgot your glasses today."

"I don't wear glasses."

"Oh, then, I guess I thought you were somebody else."

"Really? Like who?"

"Someone who didn't act freaky all the time."

"Excuse me?"

"Or went around snarking just so people would think she was cool."

Layla jumps out of her chair. "Shut up, Ashley! You have totally no right—"

"Oh, yes, I do. I can say whatever I want, Layla. I'm *improvising*."

"OKAY, STOP." Mom jumps onto the stage in one move, like a pouncing cat. "Can everyone please come onstage and make a circle? Because this is the most important session we're ever going to have."

The whole club—it looks like twenty-five kids—climbs onstage and forms a circle around Mom. She paces for a few seconds, frowning. When everyone is completely quiet, she says, "All right. What we were seeing in that scene is the *opposite* of improvisation. Because the whole basis of improv is *Yes, And*. And the only thing up on this stage just now was *No, No, No*."

"Yeah, well, Ashley and I probably shouldn't work together," Layla mutters. "We aren't *friends*, you know."

"Let me tell you something, precious students," Mom says. "Whatever negative energy is going on between you in the real world, you *never* bring it with you in front of the curtain. I did that once—I acted out a grudge onstage. And maybe it was dramatic, maybe it was funny, maybe it was the best performance I ever did. But you know what? It was also ugly. I used the stage as a personal weapon, and that's not something that should ever happen."

She takes a deep breath.

Not me. I'm not even breathing.

All the kids are watching her, but still she's just standing there. Completely still. So still she might as well be upside down, because not one single marble would be rolling.

What's she waiting for?

Ulp.

Is she about to start a performance?

Finally she presses her hands together, and speaks very slowly and carefully. "Listen, guys, there's something else I wanted to talk to you about. You are all spectacular, and I've loved every minute we've spent together. But I've decided I need to end this club. For personal reasons."

"Oh *no*," Quinn says. Her hands fly up to her mouth.

Megan glances at Ashley, whose cheeks are turning hot pink.

"But how come?" Brody says. "Why now?"

"Personal means shut up," Layla says. She looks as if she's about to cry. "Becca, I'm really so sorry about what just happened!"

"Me too," Ashley says quickly. "This whole thing was totally my fault. And I swear, from now on—"

Mom shakes her head. "It's not about today; I actually decided this last night and I told Mr. Shamsky this morning. Believe me, I really hate doing this to all of you, and on such short notice, but I have other feelings to consider. That's all I can say about it. Okay?"

No one answers.

My heart is banging so loudly I'm sure everybody can hear. But no one is looking in my direction. They're all just frozen, staring at Mom.

She holds out her arms. She's smiling, but even from back here, I can tell she's faking. "Hey, before we wrap today, group hug. The whole club."

"Do we have to?" Brody says.

"*YES,*" Layla answers, dragging him to his feet.

Then all twenty-five kids in Mom's Improv Club squish together onstage.

Which causes exactly enough commotion for me to slip out the door.

Changing the Scenes

It takes the club another ten minutes to officially break up. I'm standing in the lobby outside the auditorium watching everyone file out, but nobody stops to talk. Even Layla and Quinn are so wrapped up in their conversation that they walk right past me.

"Nothing you did," Quinn is telling Layla.

"I know she said that," Layla answers. *"But why—"*

"So unfair. This late," I hear Megan grumble.

"Yeah," Ashley tells her. *"And now we have to go sign up for some stupid—"*

When I'm sure every kid is finally gone, I slip back inside the auditorium. Mom is stacking the folding chairs onstage as if absolutely nothing has just happened.

"Oh, Mari," she says in a cheery voice. Fake-cheery. "Sorry I'm running so late today. The kids were a bit tight warming up—"

"I heard you," I blurt. "About ending the club. I was sitting in the back."

She stares. "You were?"

"Is it because of me? Is that why? Because of our fight last night?"

"Oh, baby." She smiles sadly. "That, and everything else. I've been thinking about what you've been saying, how I just keep doing the same things over and over. And you're right, I've been so selfish. It's time for me to put your feelings first. Yours and Kennie's both."

I swallow hard.

It's the line I've been waiting for her to say, I guess.

But what's funny is, now that she's actually said it, whammo, I completely change the scene on her.

"Thanks," I say. "Except my feeling is, you should do the club."

"What?"

"I saw the whole thing," I tell her. "Not just what you said at the end. You're a really good teacher."

"Well, thank you, Mari. But—"

"And I don't want you to quit."

"You're serious?"

I nod. "Promise you won't, okay?"

She rakes her sproingy hair out of her eyes. "Well, Marigold, I mean, I'm just *shocked*," she says. "Because last night you were convinced I came to Improv dripping peanut butter."

"Yeah, but then I remembered Layla's allergic. She'd challenge you to a joust if you showed up like that."

Mom stares at me.

"That's a joke," I explain. I smile at her, but she's still not smiling back.

Then I reach to touch her arm. "Listen," I say, "everyone is really psyched about this club. You should hear them in the lunchroom talking gibberish all the time. Plus there's the Mochahouse. All the parents are coming, right? You can't just not show."

"Right," Mom says slowly. "The Mochahouse." She presses her hands on my shoulders and gives me her deep-in-the-retinas look. "But Mari, you're *sure* it's okay that I'm at your school every day? Completely okay? Because I'm serious, baby, if it's not—"

"You'll know," I promise.

* * *

While Mom is off telling Mr. Shamsky that she's not quitting Improv after all, I race down the hall. Quilting Quorum is about to end for the day, and I want to be there when the end-of-after-school bell rings.

Because suddenly I realize that there's something else I need to do. Something I should have done yesterday, but maybe it's too late.

As soon as Ms. Canetti's door opens, Jada Sperry walks out, followed by Kirsten, Lexie, and Molly.

"Hey," I call out. "Jada, can I please talk to you a minute?"

She stops and narrows her eyes at me. "Sure," she says.

The eighth-grade girls stop too. Maybe they're waiting to see what happens. *Okay, fine,* I tell myself. *So I have an audience.*

"Well?" Jada says impatiently.

Go. "I was just watching my mom," I say. "And she was great. So before you say anything else about her, get your facts straight, okay?"

Jada laughs like I'm this crazy person. "What are you talking about, Marigold?"

"The Improv club. Have you seen it with your own eyes? Because maybe you just *want* it to be bad."

"Okay, you know what? This is extremely fascinating, but I really have to—"

"No, you don't," Kirsten says.

"*Excuse* me?" Jada flashes her eyes at the eighth-grade girls, but all three of them stare right back at her.

"Marigold's talking to you," Kirsten tells her. "Don't walk away; it's rude."

"Incredibly rude," Lexie agrees, and Molly nods.

Jada's face goes pale. She opens her mouth to protest, but nothing comes out.

I mean, seriously, she just looks kind of stunned. Also trapped.

And maybe it's stupid, but right now I do feel sorry for her.

And I know just what she feels like. But I blurt out: "Jada, listen. You're the last one who should be saying things about my mom. Because I heard about your parents fighting, and how everyone was talking. And that was awful for you, right? And really, really unfair. But it wasn't Quinn's fault. She couldn't help it if—"

"*Shut up, SHUT UP!*" Jada explodes. "You're not even *from* here, Marigold, so don't you *dare* talk about my family! Or anything!"

She pushes past Molly. We watch her run down the

hall, almost crashing into a group of sixth-grade soccer players.

Then Kirsten pats my back. "Nice," she says. "Even if you got a little warm and fuzzy there at the end."

"I just didn't want to be nasty," I say.

"Why not? She totally deserves it."

I shrug. There's no way I can explain how I know about Jada.

"You walking home, Marigold?" Lexie asks. "Or taking the late bus?"

"Walking," I answer. "But I'm actually waiting for someone."

She catches Molly's eye with an I-told-you-so grin. "You mean Ethan? Well, don't let *us* stop you."

And they head out just before Mom shows up with Mr. Shamsky, both of them laughing like they're old friends.

After my Big Confrontation Scene with Jada, a few major things happen.

One is that Ethan and I decide not to be secret anymore. It's not like we're all boyfriend/girlfriend in homeroom or anything, but at dismissal we meet by the flagpole and walk home together, some of the time holding hands. Brody still makes his obnoxious comments, of course, but basically we just laugh it off. Besides, the way Brody is hanging around Layla these days, it's not like he can get away with too much teasing.

Another development: The eighth-grade girls go spreading the word around school that Marigold Bailey Told Off Jada Sperry. And I don't know if it's because of that, exactly, but the permanent crowd around Jada is definitely shrinking a little. Even Ashley and Megan aren't glued to her side anymore. In fact, sometimes they sit at our table to talk about Improv, and once they even started laughing with Layla about "the time Marigold said 'squeep.'"

I guess the other main result of my Jada Scene is that I start working on the Thing in Quilting Quorum. It's like, one morning I just wake up and realize that I don't have to worry about Jada's evil eye anymore. And if Ms. Canetti doesn't understand why someone would sew a non-quilt with non-patterns, that's her problem, not mine. So I start bringing my own fabric scraps—Mom's scraps, the ones Gram sent me—from home, sewing small sections at a time. And then one day, I think, *This is stupid. I should just bring in the whole big alien-blob*. So I stuff it into my backpack, which means I have to leave a few notebooks home, but okay.

Amazingly, the eighth-grade girls love the crazy, clashing shape. Kirsten and Molly hold up a few of the corners and waft it around the classroom before Ms. Canetti shows up. "Look, it's a mutant rainbow!" Molly shouts.

"It's fabulous," Lexie gushes. "When it's open house, we should totally hang it in the front lobby."

I stop sewing. "You mean right near the main office? Are you serious?"

"Yeah. It'll make the lobby look like a psychedelic circus tent. In a good way."

"Omigod! What a fantastic idea!" Molly squeals. "I love it!"

"Listen, guys," I begin.

"You're overruled. It's three against one."

Right then Jada walks into the room and takes the seat nearest Ms. Canetti's desk. She picks up a square of fabric and immediately starts sewing, not even bothering to talk to any of us.

Which makes me feel a teeny bit guilty, actually.

But I know I can't waste more time on Jada, because now I have something new to worry about. And the thought of the whole town staring at my crazy Thing, seeing it through their own eyes, judging it, is making my stomach start to hurt.

I mean, Mom is the one who enjoys freaking out an audience. Not me.

Fireworks

"Erg, I'm so nervous," Layla says. "I think I may barf."

"Well, don't," Mom says. "I can't afford a new sofa." She squints at Layla's face, then slowly applies some eyeliner.

"Ooh, I know, Becca. Can you do Egyptian eyes? You know, thick and black, with the sides coming way, way out?"

"I can. But I won't."

"Why not?"

"Performers should never wear anything too specific. It distracts the audience."

Kennedy gives me a look. "Was that why you wouldn't

let Dad buy you a diamond ring?" she asks.

Mom smiles. "Where did you get that from?"

"Dad. That's what he told us when he gave a rock to Mona."

"Kennie," I say in a warning voice.

"It's okay, Mari," Mom says calmly. "The truth is, that's what I told him at the time. But the real reason I didn't let him buy an engagement ring is that we couldn't afford one. Two starving artists," she explains to Layla.

"Cool," Layla says, admiring her eyes in the mirror.

The doorbell rings.

"Door's open," Mom calls. "Make your entrance."

Quinn comes rushing into the living room, looking surprisingly un-babyish in her black leotard. "Sorry I'm late," she says, panting. "But my parents just got home from work, and there was all this traffic—"

"Relax, sweetheart, and save that energy for the performance." Mom studies Quinn's face a minute, then starts lining up foundations, powders, creams, eye shadows, and lipsticks all over the coffee table. She throws a towel over Quinn's shoulders and starts putting on Quinn's makeup. "Is your dad parked downstairs?"

"Across the street," Quinn says. "But he said, 'Let

Mrs. Bailey take her time with your makeup. I want you to look beautiful.'"

"Theater makeup's not for beauty," Mom corrects her. She smears on some rouge. "It's so the audience can read your expression." She outlines Quinn's lips with some liner and then puts on some lipstick, a cherry color that makes Quinn's whole face come alive.

"There," she announces. "Perfecta."

And then Beezer trots over and licks Quinn across the nose.

"Bad dog!" Mom cries. "Now I have to do a touchup."

Layla smirks at me. "When you finish, Becca, I think it's Marigold's turn."

"No, it's not," I say. "I'm not performing!"

"Au contraire," Layla argues. "Everyone's going to be looking at your quilt. And as the artist—"

"They're not going to care what my face looks like. No makeup, Layla."

"Well, you should at least change *that*," she says, pointing accusingly at my Wile E. Coyote tee.

"I like what I'm wearing," I reply. "No, wrong: I love it."

"What about nail polish?" Kennedy asks. She goes running into our bedroom and comes out with a handful of bottles.

I groan. "If I put some on, will you guys leave me alone?"

They all promise. So I grab Fun in the Sun and do two quick coats. Then we all—Mom, Kennedy, Quinn, Layla, and me—race out of the apartment and squeeze into Quinn's car, everybody laughing and talking way too loud.

"You look beautiful," Quinn's dad tells us.

"No, we don't, we look dramatic," Quinn answers. And then Layla starts doing all these silent-movie gestures that end up whacking me in the head.

"Girls, center and compose yourselves," Mom says. "Do your breathing and be calm."

"Yes, swami," Layla says.

Not me, though. The whole ride to school, my stomach feels like fireworks. The main reason is, I'm terrified what people will say about the Thing. The eighth-grade girls did exactly what they threatened to do, and convinced Ms. Canetti to display it right smack in the main lobby, so everyone has to see it. Everyone. Plus Kennedy told me that Dad called, and he said he's bringing Mona, which will make this the first time she's met Mom face-to-face. And even if Jada is wrong, and everyone isn't gossiping about Mom—whose *Birdfeeder* performance was on page five of the local newspaper— I'm sure people will talk if there's a Big Confrontation

Scene. At my school. On open house night. Truthfully, the more I think about the potential for disaster, the only thing that's keeping me from bolting when we stop for a traffic light is that Gram called an hour ago, and said she was on her way. "Cookie, I wouldn't miss this for the world," is what she said.

When we arrive in the parking lot, Mom takes Kennedy, Quinn, and Layla to the back auditorium door. Before she goes in behind them, she pulls me to her. "Can't wait to see the final version of your Thing," she says. "I'll come by the lobby after our show, okay?"

"Okay. It's not that big a deal, Mom. It's just Gram's old fabric sewn together. And you've already seen sections at home—"

"After my show," she repeats firmly. "Say break a leg."

"Break a leg. But *you're* not performing, right?"

She gives me a pretend-furious look.

"Just kidding," I say.

Then I walk into the lobby, feeling as if I'm wearing flannel monkey pajamas. On a sticky, warm June night.

I wipe my eyebrows with my sleeve.

"Marigold!" someone calls. It's Ms. Canetti. She's standing under the Thing, which the school custodian somehow tied to the overhead lights so that it looks more like a Chinese dragon than a psychedelic circus tent.

"This is our textile artist," she explains to a small crowd of parents. "Her name is Marigold Bailey, and the work is entirely her own creation."

"It's breathtaking," one woman says, grabbing my hand. "Where did you get your inspiration?"

"My what?"

"Your idea for the design."

"It doesn't really . . . have an idea. I just like how it looks."

"But didn't you mean to convey—"

"Monster? Is that you?" someone calls.

I spin around. Dad is walking toward me with Mona, who's carrying two enormous bouquets of red roses, all wrapped up with pink ribbons and baby's breath and shiny silver foil.

He nearly crushes me in a hug. Then he points up at the ceiling. "This is the quilt your grandma was telling us about?"

"It's a Thing, Dad."

"So it is. A really fantastic Thing."

"She has your eye for color, Jeff," Mona tells him.

"No, honey, she has her own eye." He waves his

hand at a tentacle-bit. "The contrasts are so electric in that section. And the shape looks almost organic, like a mysterious creature from the Great Barrier Reef."

"Thanks," I say, grinning. I suddenly remember my first day at this school, how I thought if I kept repeating the word "thanks," people would leave me alone. The funny thing is, now I'm not sure that's what I want.

"Oh, I forgot!" Mona cries. "These are for you." And she thrusts one of the giant bouquets into my arms. "I thought about getting you marigolds instead, but I don't know, they're just so puny this time of year." All of a sudden a panicky look takes over her face, like she's afraid she might have insulted me or something.

"Thanks, Mona," I say. "They're really, really beautiful." But then I start giggling. Because what else can you do when you're holding a zillion roses underneath an electric sea-dragon?

Then way down the hall, I see a familiar figure.

Two familiar figures.

"Dad?"

He nods. So I hand him the roses.

"Thanks," I manage to say, one last time.

And I race down the hall so fast it feels like I'm wearing poofy bedroom slippers.

Performance

"Mari!"

"Emma, I can't believe it's you!" I'm hugging her, she's hugging me, and we're both sort of swaying and jumping and screaming. Right in the hallway, in front of all the kids rushing to their open houses, and all their parents, and a few frantic teachers.

"But what are you doing here?" I ask, gasping.

Emma grins. "Your grandma arranged it," she says.

I look blindly at Gram, who gives me a big kiss full of magenta lipstick.

"It was really Becca's idea," Gram explains.

"Wait," I say. *"Mom's?"*

Gram nods. "Remember when I came for the weekend? Mom asked me to work on Trisha for her. She wanted to fix things, but she was afraid she'd mess up. So these past few months I've been writing letters, making phone calls, and then finally last week I paid Trisha a little visit—"

"You did?" I screech. "She let you *in?*"

Emma laughs. "She's not some dragon at the gate, Mari."

"Oh, I know! I just mean, she was so mad at Mom. About the IMs, remember? And she was so upset with *you.*"

"Well, nobody can be upset at a little old lady," Gram says, winking. "Besides, I brought her some homemade cookies. Where's Kennie?"

"Backstage with Mom."

"Shouldn't we get seats for the coffeehouse?"

"*Mochahouse.* Kennie's saving some for us. And for Dad and Mona." I blink at Emma. "I'm just in total . . . shock."

"So snap out of it," Gram says, squeezing my hand. "And let's take a stroll over to look at the Thing."

A half hour later, we're in the third row of the auditorium: Dad, Mona, Kennedy, Gram, Emma, and me.

Two rows ahead of us—the first row, dead center, are Jada and her mother. And Ethan is sitting with his parents three rows back; we wave at each other, but I guess neither one of us feels ready to be un-secret in front of our families. Plus about two hundred of our friends and classmates.

But Emma sees the wave. "Who's that?" she whispers.

"Boyfriend," I whisper back.

"Really?"

"Yeah."

She cranes her neck and stares at him. "Ooh la la," she says, and then we both start giggling so hard Gram leans over and slaps my knee.

The lights dim, and Mom comes out onstage in her chocolate cake leotard.

"Welcome to our Mochahouse," she says in her perfect stage voice. "What you're about to see is a program we call *Actors at Play*. All of the students chose their own performances. Some are improvs, some are not, but all of them use theater techniques we explored this spring in our club. We'd like to thank Lisa Sperry and the Crampton PTA for all their support, and we hope to see many of you again next spring. And now, enjoy."

The program starts. You can tell that some of it kind of confuses the audience—like when Ashley and Megan sit onstage facing each other, playing Emotional Mirror, or when Brody burps to the tune of *Star Wars*. But Layla's performance as a trash-talking knight challenging audience members to joust is a big hit. And when Quinn stands at the microphone and sings "Defying Gravity," it brings down the house.

"Whoa," Emma whispers. "That girl can *sing*."

"She's one of my best friends," I whisper back. "But really, I had no idea."

When the applause dies down, Mom steps to the mic. "Wasn't Quinn great?" she asks, and then there's a second round of clapping. When *that* finally stops, Mom smiles. "Okay," she says. "I guess this wouldn't be an improv show without some audience participation. Does anyone here tonight have a scene they'd like us to perform?"

People titter. Or mumble. No one shouts anything.

In the first row a hand goes up. Jada's.

Mom points at her eagerly. "Yes?"

"Mrs. Bailey," Jada says in a supersweet voice, "would *you* do a performance for us?"

No. NO.

"Oh, I couldn't," Mom says, smiling. "This isn't my evening."

"Oh, but *please?*"

Someone starts to clap. Then three people. Then, like, ten.

My insides dry up. My head starts to buzz. In all the disasters I'd imagined for tonight, I never imagined this. NO, I tell myself. I CAN'T LET HER DO THIS. NOT HERE. NOT TONIGHT. NOT IN FRONT OF EMMA AND JADA AND JADA'S MOM. AND ALSO ETHAN AND MONA AND, *LIKE, THE ENTIRE TOWN.*

NONONONONO.

I stand up.

"What are you doing?" Emma hisses. She grabs my arm.

"Marigold?" Kennedy asks in a scared voice.

I don't answer. I stare at the stage. At the lights. At Mom.

Then I call out in a voice that isn't mine, *"Mom? Can I do a scene with you?"*

"Mari?" she breathes into the mic.

I never saw Mom look frozen on a stage before, but for one split second she's entirely still. White-faced.

In shock. Then her face breaks out in a grin. "Oh, yes! Let's all have a round of applause for my brave daughter, Marigold!"

"Oh, Lord," I hear Gram say.

The audience starts clapping, and as I'm climbing up to the stage, I'm thinking, *THIS IS A DREAM. I'M PROBABLY JUST SLEEPWALKING.* I dig my thumbnails into my palms and try to wake up.

But I don't.

Now somehow I've arrived onstage, the lights in my eyes, my legs soft like overcooked spaghetti. No, Twizzlers. Twizzlers left overnight on the radiator. And not stiff from Joy.

I look straight out: The audience is smeary blobs of color, not really faces I can read. That's probably a good thing.

I look left and right: The whole club is gathered in the theater wings looking shocked. Horrified. *Not* a good thing.

Okay, so what do I do now?

"Go, Marigold!" somebody hollers. It sounds like Kirsten.

Somebody else whistles.

"Whoo-hoo!" Lexie shouts.

I stare frantically at Mom.

She puts her hands on my shoulders as if to keep me from floating away. Then she looks deep into my eyes. "Let's chat about the Thing," she murmurs. "Okay, baby?"

I nod. *This will be fine,* I tell myself. *Just fine. As long as I don't have to talk. Or breathe.*

Mom drags two chairs to the center of the stage. She gently pushes me into one, and takes the other. Then she sits very straight and cocks her head to one side, like a perky TV anchorwoman. "Greetings," she says in a loud, cheerful voice. "We're here today chatting with the famous Thing-artist Marigold Bailey. Marigold—if I may be so bold as to call you that— you've worked on this project for a very long time, haven't you?"

I swallow.

Nothing.

Still nothing.

I'm nothing but a giant sweaty eyebrow.

"According to my research, you began this"—she flips imaginary cards—"several months ago, isn't that right?"

I can see the *come-on-Marigold-you-can-do-it* look in

her eye. I feel her energy radiating in my direction, like waves of heat.

"Squeep," I answer.

The audience rustles. A few people laugh.

"*What* did she say?" somebody's grandfather asks loudly.

Becca Bailey doesn't blink. "Drotella goobaba frew trayko meenen," she replies cheerfully, checking something off on her imaginary index card. And then on we go, back and forth, the whole interview in total gibberish. Actually, she does most of the talking; my answers are basically monosyllables. But at least I get them out; at least it's an actual back-and-forth conversation. And by the end of the two minutes or so, I'm watching her in amazement: Not only is she conducting the interview with me, she's also cutting away to do commercials. And the news and weather. Every time in different gibberish-languages, if that even makes sense.

Finally she springs up. Which means our scene is over, so I stand up too. And then the audience starts applauding like crazy, and Dad starts throwing roses at the stage. Kennedy throws a few, and so does Emma, and pretty soon Mom and I are standing there ducking roses and tossing them back into the audience. Then

Mom beckons for the whole Improv Club to come out and take a bow, so we all hug each other and laugh and toss roses and wave at the audience, and then the lights come on and suddenly the whole thing is over.

"THANKS FOR COMING!" Mom shouts into the mic. "STOP BY THE LOBBY ON THE WAY OUT, AND BE SURE TO CHECK OUT MARIGOLD'S THING."

"Omigod!" I scream at Layla, who's squeezing me and jumping up and down.

"Dude, I can't believe you did that!" she shrieks.

"Neither can I."

"You were amazing."

"So were you! And Quinn! And everybody else!"

"And Becca *rocked.* The way she did all those voices—"

"I know! By the end she almost had me relaxed. *Almost.*"

That's when I suddenly realize: I was onstage with Mom during one of her performances. And she knew who I was. She knew *exactly* who I was, and somehow, in some crazy way I never expected, the two of us built a scene together.

And it worked.

* * *

Probably because of the free publicity from the Mochahouse, a ton of people troop over to the lobby and say nice gushy stuff about the Thing. The best part about all this attention is that it means I get to introduce Emma to everybody. And when Mom gives her an enormous hug, I can tell she's not surprised to see her here. (And why would she be? Working on Trisha was her idea, Gram said.)

"Wasn't Marigold *spectacular*?" she shouts at Emma. "And don't you love this fantastic Thing?"

"Yes," Emma says, laughing. "To both questions."

Even Ethan comes over. He chats with Emma for a minute, and then says to me, "Uh, Marigold? Can I talk to you in private?"

So I tell Emma I'll be right back, and step into the nurse's office with Ethan.

"You okay?" I ask him.

"Um, yeah," he says. "I just wanted to say you did great. And."

"And what?" I ask.

Dead silence.

"And what?" I repeat.

He kisses me quickly. He smells like Dentyne.

"Okay, Marigold?" he asks, stepping backward.

I grin. "Yeah. Okay, Ethan."

That night, after Dad and Mona leave, and the rest of us are back in the apartment, I put on my yellow flannel monkey pajamas, the ones I swore I'd never wear again. Kennedy offers to sleep in the living room with Gram, so Emma and I have the bedroom to ourselves. The first thing we do is our toes and fingers. Fun in the Sun has already started to chip, so I polish us both with Juicy Passionfruit. Three glossy coats, one after the other, first hers, then mine.

And we talk until two in the morning. About school and all our friends. About Ethan and Will (who Emma doesn't like as much as this new boy, Jake). About our moms. About ourselves.

When it's finally time to turn out the lights, Emma says softly from Kennedy's bed, "Mari? I'm really sorry."

"What for?"

"You know. What happened. Giving up on our friendship."

"It wasn't your fault," I tell her. "I know things were really hard at your house."

"That's not an excuse. I totally messed up, didn't I?"

She doesn't wait for an answer. "So were you incredibly mad?"

"Yeah. But not at you." I smile. "Can I say something, Emma?"

"Uh-huh."

"You shouldn't be so afraid of fighting, you know? Sometimes it's better than *not* fighting. As long as it ends." Even in the dark, my nails catch the light, and I can see the tips shining. Perfect. "Anyway, I'm just glad we're over all that. I really, really missed you."

"I missed you, too. You're still my best friend."

"You're still mine," I say. Then I add, "I have other friends too. Some great ones, actually."

"Yeah, they seem nice." She pauses. "So we're back to before?"

"No," I say. "No, I think we're better now."

The next morning, Mom makes us all some cinnamon muffins, and allows Gram to take Beezer out for Morning Walk. ("*Whose* dog is this?" Gram demands. Mom laughs. "Ours, I guess," she admits.) Emma and I make plans for me spending a week with her family on Cape Cod. And we promise to talk on the phone every Saturday. At the absolute least.

Just before lunch, she and Gram leave for their bus.

"Thank you," I say in Gram's ear. "For everything."

"Talk to your mom," she whispers in mine. "Tell her where I got all that fabric."

"You think she'll remember? It was so long ago."

"It wasn't really." She kisses my forehead. "Talk to her, Mari. Just sit down, the two of you, and talk."

So we do.

Get a special look at another
great book by
Barbara Dee:

this is me from now on

I took off my flip-flops and walked into the living room, which was always the nippiest room in the house.

Francesca Pattison was sitting in what Mom calls the loveseat. I didn't really focus on her at first—I was too busy staring at her aunt Samantha. It was one of the few times I'd seen Samantha Pattison in daylight. Mostly my sister and I had just peeked at her late at night slamming the door of a black BMW convertible, and then clattering up her driveway in noisy, high-heeled shoes. None of us could figure out why a thirty-fivish woman with no kids and an obviously amazing social life would choose to live in our nice but extremely nonamazing subdivision. Samantha Pattison was something to talk about when we needed a topic at the dinner table.

And now here she was sipping Diet Snapple with my mom, looking normal and suburban in a yellow flowered sundress and sandals. "So grateful," I heard her saying as I plopped into a squishy armchair.

"Hi, honey. You remember our neighbor, Ms. Pattison?" Mom said, giving me a look.

"Oh, sure," I lied, because how could I remember someone I'd never even officially met? "Hi."

"And this is her niece Francesca." Mom turned to where Francesca was sitting, but she wasn't there anymore. Now she was standing by our big bookshelf, pulling down book after book.

The first thing I thought about her was: *Omigod. That girl is a giant. Is she taller than Dad? I think she is.*

"Your books are so BRILLIANT," she was practically shouting. "*Wuthering Heights*—I *love* this book! It's the most gorgeous book ever written. Can I borrow it?"

"We can borrow books from the Blanton Library," her aunt Samantha said. "Say hello to Eva."

"Evie," I said automatically.

"Francesca is entering seventh grade too," Mom said, smiling. "She's a sort of transfer student."

"Oh, really? From where?" I asked.

"The depths of hell," Francesca answered.

Samantha Pattison giggled, rattling her ice cubes. "You don't mean that, sugarpie."

"Oh yes I do."

"Why? What was wrong with your old school?" I asked.

"Everything," Francesca said, looking right at me as if she were confessing some top secret. "They tried to suppress my spirit, but of course they failed miserably."

The second thing I thought was: *Whoa. That girl looks incredible. I wish my hair was long and all wavy like that, and my eyes were that smoky sort of green. And I bet SHE doesn't have trouble finding a bathing suit!* The third thing was: *On the other hand, she's crazy.*

"Evie, honey," Mom said, "why don't you get yourself some lemonade, and then maybe you could take Francesca over to see Blanton Middle."

"You mean right now?"

"Oh, that's not necessary, Mrs. Webber," said Francesca. "I prefer not to think about school. It's not for ages, anyway."

Mom smiled. "Actually, it's less than a week away. In Blanton we start school in late August."

"Then we still have eons," Francesca answered cheerfully. "But I'd absolutely love a walk, Evie, if you really wouldn't mind."

"I wouldn't mind," I said, looking helplessly at Mom. "It's just incredibly hot out there."

"That's all right," Francesca said. "I've been living in Saudi Arabia. I'm used to extreme temperatures."

"Francesca's dad is in the oil business," Samantha Pattison explained.

"Oh." I knew I was supposed to be impressed by that, but I didn't even know what "the oil business" meant, exactly. I looked at Francesca. "You want some lemonade too?"

"No thanks," she said. "I've already had three absolutely scrumptious glasses."

Okaaaay, I thought. I went into the kitchen and got myself a glass of ice cubes surrounded by lemonade. Grace, my school-aholic big sister, was sitting at the dining room table hunched over a book called *Acing the SAT.* She filled in a test bubble and looked up at me, grinning. "Samantha Pattison," she said.

"I know. In broad daylight."

"With her niece."

"I know. Did you meet her? She seems—"

"Not now," murmured Grace, raising her eyebrows.

"Are you ready, Evie?" someone said from behind me. Francesca clomped into the dining room. That's when I noticed she was wearing a normal-looking outfit (purple tank top, green shorts) but also these pointy-toed, sparkly blue stilettos with, like, four-inch super-skinny heels.

I swear, when I saw those shoes I practically choked on an ice cube. Because I'd never seen anything like them in my entire life; I had no idea what I was supposed to think about them. It was like a quiz from one of Lily's magazines:

> **What's your take on Francesca's shoes?**
> (a) Soooo tacky—*What was she thinking?*
> (b) Soooo babyish—*Is she channeling Cinderella?*
> (c) Soooo weird—*Do they wear those things on Neptune?*
> (d) Soooo hot—*I wonder if they'd fit me!*

And here's the funny part: I realized I was thinking all four things at the same time. So maybe the right answer was (e) All of the above. Even if that wasn't a choice.

Now Francesca clomped over to Grace. "What are you doing?" she asked, trying to read upside down.

"Studying for the SAT," Grace answered.

"But it's only August. Why worry about some bloody awful test before school even starts?"

Grace smiled in this superior way she has. "Well, I'm a senior in high school. Going to be. And if I want to go to a good college, I need to take the SAT this fall."

"How *sad*," said Francesca. "That's why I absolutely refuse to go to college, among other reasons. Well, don't let us distract you." Then her face brightened. "Unless you'd like to come with us? We're going for a nice long walk."

"That's okay," Grace said, catching my eye. "Have fun, you two." She picked up a pencil and flipped a page in her SAT book, pretending not to laugh.

I squinted at Francesca. Even outside in the glaring sunshine she looked fantastic: her skin was a golden tan, and her hair was the color of Kraft Caramels. "So where do you want to go?" I asked, my teeth skidding on the last little slivers of ice cubes.

"Oh, you decide," Francesca said happily. "You're the expert."

"I am?"

"Well, you live here, don't you? Where do you go when you want to have fun?"

"I don't know. The mall, probably. When someone's mom can drive us."

She made a face. "Where else?"

"The park. The movies. The stores on Elm."

"Blah. Boring."

"The ice cream place—"

"Ooh, ice cream," she said, clapping her hands. "What a genius idea. Is it far?"

"Sort of. Half a mile, maybe."

"Oh, that's nothing. I love to walk."

I looked at her feet. "Even in those shoes? They don't look very comfortable."

"Oh, they're not. They're bloody torture, actually. But they're so epically gorgeous, don't you think?" She took off her left shoe. I could see the side of her foot near her big toe looked pink and peely. She rubbed it, then put the shoe right back on and beamed at me. "Besides, if Mother Darling saw me wearing them, she'd go berserk. So who cares about stupid blisters."

I didn't know what to say to that; it never occurred to me to *want* my mom to go berserk. The truth is, Mom went berserk all the time, over things like unwashed dishes and unmade beds, and I didn't exactly find it entertaining. And why did Francesca just call her own mom 'Mother Darling'? She talked really, really strangely, like everything she said was in quotation marks or something.

We walked long blocks without saying very much.

The air was so hot, it was almost chewy, and I could feel the sweat trickling down my armpits, even though this morning I'd snuck some of Grace's powder-fresh deodorant. Francesca was definitely limping by now. Once or twice I saw her stop and rub her foot, but she never complained or took her shoe off again. Finally she pointed across the street. "Is that the ice cream place, Evie? It looks like heaven."

"I wouldn't go that far," I said. "But I really like their chocolate chip."

She wiped her forehead. "Yum, chocolate chip. My absolute favorite."

We crossed the street and went inside. Oh, I should tell you that I Scream for Ice Cream (I know, I know: dumb name) was owned by Zane's dad, and Zane helped out there sometimes. Today was one of those days, probably because the place was packed with sticky first graders off the camp bus and moms sick of dieting all summer to fit into bathing suits and middle schoolers in denial about the end of vacation.

We got in line. As soon as we did, the door opened again, and two girls I knew from school walked in: Kayla and Gaby. Definitely cooler-than-me types, but I'd say lower-medium-nice.

"Hey, Evie," said Kayla, finger-combing her fakely highlighted long brown hair. "What Team are you on? Hard or Easy?"

"I don't know. I haven't read my letter yet." This was true; I'd gotten my Seventh-Grade Team Assignment Letter last week, but I'd just stuffed it into my desk drawer.

Kayla smiled like she didn't believe me. "We're both on Hard. What about Nisha and Lily?"

"Hard," I said. "Like always."

"Poor them," Gaby commented. "Hard has Espee."

I nodded. Oh yes, I knew all about the Espee business. When my sister, Grace, took seventh-grade U.S. History, all she did—I mean literally, ALL SHE DID—was research and write bibliographies, sometimes until two in the morning. Her social life basically ended that year; the only thing she cared about was satisfying this insatiable monster she referred to as SP. I was, like, seven years old then, so I thought "SP" stood for something too horrible to call a teacher out loud, like Scary Person or Sour Pickle. Finally I asked Grace what SP meant, and she said, "Stephanie Pierce. She signs everything SP, so that's what we call her." "To her *face*?" I'd asked. "Of course not," Grace had said, hooting at my stupidity. "She'd vaporize you."

Francesca, who I *could* have introduced at that point, was standing on her tippy-toes, even though she was nearly six feet tall with those all-of-the-above shoes. "What does that sign say?" she asked too loudly. "Mochaccino Supremo? What's that?" And then she turned around and grinned at me. "Deeply gorgeous boy. Behind the counter."

In back of me, Gaby started giggling. I've always hated the way she sounded when she laughed, kind of like a car alarm.

"That's Zane," Kayla announced. "He's in eighth grade."

"Zane," Francesca repeated still-too-loudly. "What an odd name." Then she stared at me with her huge, smoky green eyes. "You're in love with him, Evie, aren't you?"

"What?"

"I'm psychic about these things. I should have warned you."

"Yes? Next in line?" Zane called out.

"Oops, my turn!" Francesca walked right up to Zane, gave him a dazzling smile, and asked, "So, Zane, what do you recommend?"

I could have died. What did he *recommend?* Gah. Didn't she even know how to order ice cream like a normal human being? I could hear Gaby and Kayla laughing, maybe about Francesca, maybe about me. And then I saw Zane hand Francesca a tiny plastic spoon and one of those little paper cups they used for free samples.

Francesca took a spoonful of whatever-it-was. "Ooh, lovely," she said. She pointed to some other kind of ice cream in the case. "What's that?"

"Triple Fudge Marshmallow Chunk. Try it," said Zane, handing her another paper cup.

"Yumyumyum," said Francesca when she'd taken a bite. "What's that?"

He read the label upside down. "Um, Golden Brownie with Caramel Fudge Ripple."

Francesca clutched her chest like she was having a heart attack.

So Zane handed her another free sample.

"Bliss," Francesca said. "I've never tasted anything so epically delish!"

"Aaaa, come on, dude, we're waiting here," snarled some high-school-looking boy three customers behind me.

"Be right with you," Zane answered. But he just kept handing Francesca free sample after free sample. And

Francesca just kept pointing at the ice cream freezer and saying "lovely" and "yummy" and "Ooh, what's that?" Finally a grouchy mom with one of those sticky camp kids called out, "Excuse me, but is this line ever *moving?*" And then the sticky camp kid yelled at her, "Mommy, you said I could have ice cream *NOW!*"

I felt a jabbing poke on my shoulder.

"Hey, Evie, aren't you with that girl?" Kayla was asking.

"Who?"

She tilted her highlights toward Francesca. "*Her.* The one eating up half the freezer."

"Her name is Francesca," I said. I was about to add, "I don't even know her," but I stopped myself. After all, they'd heard her call me Evie; they'd almost definitely also heard about her psychic powers.

Suddenly, Sticky Camp Kid started screaming his head off, and Grouchy Mom was telling him, "You'll get your ice cream in TWO MORE MINUTES, buddy," like it was a threat aimed right at Zane, and I thought: *Okay. If I don't do something NOW, Francesca Pattison is going to start a riot in here. Everyone in this line is going to leap into that freezer and start scooping ice cream with their bare hands. And maybe throwing it at her like snowballs.* And even though walking over to Francesca was like posting on YouTube that we had some kind of official connection, at this point I really didn't think I had too much of a choice.

So I went over to her. She was pointing at a melty-looking tub of Rainbow Cotton Candy. "Ooh, *that* looks interesting," she was commenting to Zane. Then she noticed me. "Have you ever tried that flavor, Evie?"

"Not really. But I bet it's great." I added under my breath, "Just order something, Francesca. Okay?"

"Are you all right?" she asked me, scrunching up her forehead like she was worried about my health.

"Yes! Just *please, please* hurry up."

"Oh, sure." She put her tiny paper cup and her plastic spoon on the counter, smiled at Zane, and said, "It's all spectacular, Zane. But I'm afraid I'm absolutely stuffed. I'll have to come back for a cone some other time."

He blinked his gold-hazel eyes. "You mean you're not buying anything?"

"Oh, *no* thank you. But Evie will, I think."

We watched her clomp to the door.

"I'll have a chocolate chip cone," I said quickly. "Single scoop, please."

When Zane handed it to me, our knuckles sort of

banged into each other, and it shocked me just how freezing his hand was. I mean, he was scooping ice cream all day; *of course* his hand would be icy cold. But it made me feel weird, like I wanted to run home and knit him some gloves. And the crazy thing is, I don't even knit.

So instead I reached into my pocket and gave him every bit of money I had—four dollars and fifty-three cents.

"That's for Francesca too," I said. Then brilliantly I added, "Uh, sorry, Zane."

"No problem," he muttered. I watched him stuff the money in the register without even counting it. Then he did this cool little head-jerk to toss his long, wavy bangs out of his face. "Next?"

"Bye, Evie, see you at school!" Gaby called out.

"What school?" I answered. I grabbed a fistful of napkins and walked out into the scorching heat.

Francesca was standing right in front of the door, shading her eyes. "What kind did you get? Chocolate chip? I adore that flavor. It's my absolute favorite!"

"You said that before." Already it was starting to drip down the sides of my cone, so I licked it fast. "Then why didn't you get any?"

"Because . . . well, chocolate chip is always exactly the same." She did that heart-clutching thing again. "And there were so many other flavors. And they all looked so scrumptious. Evie, don't you ever get *utterly bored*—"

"No." I wrapped a napkin around the soggy cone. "The thing is, Francesca, I'm pretty sure Zane thought you'd pick a flavor. Eventually. And then pay him for it."

She looked shocked. "Oh, I would have. But of course I couldn't."

"Why not?"

"Because I don't have any money." She pulled out her shorts pockets. They were totally empty. "See?" she said, smiling sweetly.

Okay. Okay. I had *no idea* what I was supposed to say to that. Because what did she think she was doing just now? Ice cream research? And why hadn't she just told me that on the way over? I'd have loaned her some money; I'd pretty much paid for her anyway. I mean, I didn't even know what to *think* about a person who could act the way she just had.

And in front of so many people. Including people I knew. People I'd be going to school with in just a few more days.

Gah. It was just too horrible. And embarrassing. And weird. So for the entire walk home I tried really, really hard to tune her out. She was going on and on about some gelato place she went to once in Rome or something, but I just made myself think about Zane, and whether or not he blamed *me,* and also how much longer I could go without opening my Team Letter. And I concentrated extremely hard on my lopsided ice cream cone, trying to catch the drips before they splattered on the sidewalk.

Barbara Dee knows what tweens like!
Collect every one of her M!X books.

Just Another Day
in My Insanely Real Life

Solving Zoe

This Is Me From Now On

From Aladdin • Published by Simon & Schuster